# SCANDALOUS BILLIONAIRE

SIERRA CARTWRIGHT

SCANDALOUS BILLIONAIRE

Copyright @ 2020 Sierra Cartwright

First E-book Publication: February 2020

Line Editing by Jennifer Barker

Diversity Editing by Renita McKinney, A Book a Day

Proofing by Bev Albin and Cassie Hess-Dean

Cover Design by Rachel Connolly

Photographer: Annie Ray/Passion Pages

Cover Model: Caleb Johnson

Photo provided by © Annie Ray/Passion Pages

Promotion by Once Upon An Alpha/Shannon Hunt

All rights reserved. Except for use in a review, no part of this publication may be reproduced, distributed, or transmitted in any form, or by any means, electronic or mechanical, including photocopying, recording, or by any information storage and retrieval system, without prior written permission of the author.

This is a work of fiction. Names, characters, places, brands, media, and incidents are either the products of the author's imagination or are used fictitiously, and any resemblance to any actual persons, living or dead, is entirely coincidental.

The author acknowledges the trademarked status and trademark owners of various products referenced in this work of fiction. The publication/use of these trademarks is not authorized, associated with, or sponsored by the trademark owners.

Adult Reading Material

Disclaimer: This work of fiction is for mature (18+) audiences only and contains strong sexual content and situations.

It is a standalone with my guarantee of satisfying happily ever after.

All rights reserved.

## DEDICATION

*BAB, there really are no words to express what it's been like to have you along for every step of the journey over the past years. You're so valued.*
*Jen, thank you, thank you for being so great to work with.*
*Renita, you are amazing! I admire your talent tremendously. Your suggestions are spot on and very much appreciated.*
*And to you. I appreciate your taking the time to drop me a line to say hello and share your stories with me.*

CHAPTER ONE

"What in the fuck do you think you're doing?"

The woman in his bedroom closet gasped and swung around, clutching his red tie against her chest. Her eyes—the stunning blue of a topaz—were wide open, and her mouth was parted in shock. For a moment, he could do nothing but stare. Her full, kissable lips were painted red. *Red?* No. It wasn't red. More like scarlet, the color of temptation.

He had an instant response to the sweet, springlike scent of her, until—

*Jesus.*

"Lizzie?" Braden blinked. It took him a moment to place her. He knew her, but at first he hadn't recognized her at all.

For most of his early years, Elizabeth Ryan had been a fixture in his house. She was the daughter of his housekeeper —*the much younger, off-fucking-limits* daughter of his housekeeper, he mentally amended.

A few years ago, she'd gone away to college, and he hadn't seen her since.

But now, she was back, more beautiful than ever,

standing in his closet, near the shelves that held his shoes and winter sweaters.

"Braden." She remained in place, as if shock had momentarily paralyzed her. "I..."

While he waited for her to go on, he swept his gaze over her. In the past four years, she'd changed considerably. Her cheekbones were more pronounced. Her curves were fuller, more enticing. But still, even in heels, she wouldn't reach his chin.

She cleared her throat and tried again. "I wasn't expecting you."

"Obviously." It wasn't often that he escaped the office to come home in the middle of the day, but if he were guaranteed to find her in his bedroom, that might change. *Shit.* What the hell was he thinking? This was Lizzie he was lusting over. He shook his head to get rid of the outrageous thought. "Care to explain yourself?"

"Ah... My mom recruited me to help her out. You know, for tomorrow's party. There's a lot to be done still, and she needs the help."

Braden nodded. Lucky him, tomorrow he was hosting his grandparents' seventieth anniversary party. A year ago, his mother had announced the event would be held here, at his house. Her royal decree hadn't surprised him. His grandparents had built the River Oaks mansion in Houston in the 1950s, with an eye toward entertaining.

In the previous century, pictures of the numerous Gallagher soirees graced the newspaper society pages. But now, his grandfather's health was declining. While he was still strong enough, they wanted one last magnificent party.

And Lizzie was right—there was a lot still to finish up, even though there'd been constant banging and clanging on the property for more than a week. Massive air-conditioned tents had been erected. All the pool decking had been power washed. A hundred potted plants and palms had been wheeled in. Fairy lights—how they were different than any other damn thing, he didn't know—draped from his live oak tree and were threaded through all the fencing. As if that wasn't enough, there were numerous lanterns flickering.

Almost all of the furniture from the main level had been moved into storage—the dining room set belonging to his grandparents, as well as the contemporary pieces he preferred. Rugs had been rolled up and hauled out, and pocket doors had been pushed all the way open so that the living room and parlor became a ballroom, as per the home's original design.

Tall tables had been brought in and draped with white cloths and adorned with floating candles—since he had no idea what they were, he'd take the party planner's word for it—and tiny vases of flowers. All of that had been irksome, but not as annoying as the hammering and pounding as a stage for the quartet had been erected. If he was smarter, he would have moved to a hotel for a couple of weeks.

However, none of the preparation explained why the very attractive Lizzie Ryan was in his closet. "As far as I know, my grandparents aren't planning to give private tours of the master bedroom. *My* bedroom."

"You're right, of course." Her face was scarlet, and she held his tie in a death grip. "I'll just…"

He waited a full ten seconds before prompting, "You'll just…?"

"Finish up here."

"I asked what you were doing, Lizzie."

"I heard you. I was ignoring you and the question." She took a step back, but the shelving halted any further retreat. For as long as he wanted, she was trapped.

A pulse hammered in her throat, and it was maddening how much he liked it.

Braden moved toward her with purposeful intent, only stopping when he was mere inches from her. Desire, as carnal as it was forbidden, plowed into him. "Do you often trespass when I'm not here, Lizzie?"

"I..." Her voice cracked, and she took a breath to compose herself. Then, after a few seconds, her tone even, she went on. "This is the first time."

That was probably the truth; after all, she hadn't been here in years. At least not that he knew of. That didn't stop him from fantasizing, just for a moment, that she'd been here before.

No doubt his imaginings were nefarious and her reason for being in his bedroom was innocent.

She extended her arms, holding the tie between them as a physical barrier as she explained herself. "It was under the couch in your living room."

Was that where he'd dropped it? Then he remembered. Jennifer Pollis. The evening had been interesting. Well, right up until the moment that she mentioned the ways she might want to remodel the kitchen.

Immediately he'd dressed and fetched her purse. Even as she protested, he'd called for a driver to take her home.

"Instead of telling my mother where I found this, I decided to put it away myself. You *could* thank me for doing you a favor, but you won't."

He wondered how that quip didn't draw blood. There was no doubt she'd grown up. In front of him was a confident woman, unimpressed by his money or...frankly, him.

Truthfully he shouldn't be embarrassed that it was obvious he'd had sex in the living room. He was a grown man, and it was his house. And still, it did make him uncomfortable that she'd been the one to find it.

With her chin tipped back, she looked at him. "There's

plenty of work still to be done this evening. If you'll excuse me?"

She shoved the tie at him.

"Did you try my drawers?" What the hell was wrong with him? He should let her go. But he had to know what she'd seen, and she was making no attempt to get past him.

Something was happening here, and he wasn't sure what the hell it was. He was caught in an undertow, and he wanted to take her down with him. "Did you?"

"Yes." The word was part whisper, part confession.

God help him, it made him hungry to hear vulgar words fall from her beautiful mouth. "So you discovered it doesn't go in my top drawer, with my underwear." The relatively few pair he wore. Mostly tight-fitting and moisture wicking for when he worked out. "Or in the second one, with my socks."

She nodded.

"Did you open the one after that?"

"You came in before I got that far." Her answer was quick. Far too quick.

Lizzie, the girl who'd become a desirable woman, was a pretty little liar. The way she glanced at the dresser—nervously and repeatedly—proved it. "Maybe you should see if that's where it goes."

"*No.*"

He grinned, a lightning-fast, triumphant response that he failed to hide. "So you do know what's in there. You saw them, didn't you?" The floggers, restraints, blindfolds, gags. And no doubt, also the rope that would wrap exquisitely around her tiny middle.

"Look, Braden, I'm here to help my mother with a very big job. It was never my intention to invade your privacy."

"Lizzie. Lizzie. We both know the truth. It started that way. But it turned into snooping. It makes me wonder why."

The scarlet flush deepened.

"I have a tie rack." He reached over to push a button nestled on the wall. A board filled with neat, flat U-shaped hooks slid out. "For future reference, it goes there." He hung it in place, right above a selection of whips and paddles.

"Uhm. I'll be sure to remember that if I ever find your clothes on the floor after you've had a night of debauchery."

"I'm not sure I've ever heard anyone use that word." It was as brave as the tilt of her chin.

If she'd been scandalized when she opened his third drawer, she would have dropped the tie and run. Instead, she'd stayed. "Are you in the least bit curious?"

"Not at all. You have kinks. And that's okay. They're nothing to be ashamed of."

*"Ashamed?"* He sure as fuck was not. "A taste for BDSM, a little tie-me-up, tie-me-down is fine, as long as it's between consenting adults."

"Agreed. No argument from me. As a member of your staff, you can count on my discretion."

That was the last thing he wanted from her. "Stop the bullshit. You're not staff."

"Your signature is on my mother's paycheck." Her shoulders were straighter, as if she'd donned an invisible set of armor. "She serves at your pleasure, and I don't want to jeopardize that."

"Over you being in my closet? You think I'd fire someone who's essential to my family, who has been with me since I was a child, who at times was more caring than my own mother..." Anger seared, fed by Lizzie's thoughtless insensitivity. Her mother, Eileen Ryan, had wiped his tears, helped him through his grief, showed up once for a parent-teacher conference after his dad had left and his mother was in bed for the third day in a row and he, a nine-year-old, hadn't understood why. "What the fuck kind of man do you think I am?"

"You have a reasonable expectation of privacy in your own home, even when your housekeeper—"

Lizzie's soothing, placating tone pissed him off.

"Honestly, Braden, all I wanted to do was put your tie back where it belonged. Not cause upset."

He'd fucking heard enough.

Braden grabbed her by the shoulders and pulled her up, until her prim-and-proper little heels were inches off the hardwood floor. "Don't you ever, ever say anything like that again."

Her mouth parted, and she sucked a tiny breath.

"Your mother can work here as long as she wants. She's more than a damn employee to me, and you know it." A lifetime ago, he and Lizzie had sat across the kitchen island from each other, drinking milk and eating chocolate chip cookies after school. But now, this woman had the face and body of a goddess, and she was cursed with the tongue of a hellion. "You've dealt me the greatest insult I've ever received."

"Braden—"

With his mouth, his kiss, his absolute fucking anger, he silenced her.

He used his tongue to press past her sealed lips, seeking entrance.

Braden knew what polite society said behind his back. That he was rich, privileged from birth. That his behavior was, at best, scandalous. At worst, reckless.

But he'd never had the one thing he needed most. Love. Others received it, but it had never been meant for him.

His life experiences had hardened him. To cope, he'd walled off his emotions. Despite that, he thought the world of women, and he enjoyed spoiling them with meals and gifts, and sex. His particular fondness was for BDSM. The sweet sigh of a submissive's surrender was the most beautiful sound in the world.

He'd been careful to never make promises, and he didn't utter careless words of affection. One date accused him of being emotionally cold. She'd been right.

But in under five minutes, Lizzie had pissed him off and simultaneously intrigued him.

At first, he tasted the tang of her resistance. Her eyes were wide, and she kept her body rigid. And then...

He softened the kiss.

He no longer wanted to punish her thoughtless words. Instead he hungered to know more about her. Was she as passionate as she was standoffish? Was she at all curious about what she'd found in his closet? Would her capitulation be as mind-blowing as he imagined it might be?

In his arms, Lizzie moaned. It was soft, more a whimper than anything, and yet it stoked the flame inside him.

He pulled her closer and tasted her deeper. She no longer resisted him. Instead, she leaned into him.

Braden was there for her, pressing one hand to the small of her back. With the other he tugged the pin from her hair and sent her brunette tresses cascading over her shoulders and down her back.

She was the sexiest woman he'd ever had in his arms.

Earlier, she might have had a glass of wine. There was sweetness from the grapes, and perhaps the drying bitterness of tannins all rolled into one and wrapped in her response.

Like a dying man, he was mad for more.

Braden plundered her mouth, and as the moments passed, she linked her hands behind his neck and offered herself to him.

She met his thrust with her parry. What they shared was heated with an intensity unlike any other, threatening him with combustion.

He wanted surrender as much as her demands.

Finally, when neither could breathe, he pulled back a little. But even that was too much. Instantly, he claimed her mouth again, and her blazing response seared him.

She kissed him back, as demanding as he'd been. She wasn't the aggressor. Not at all. Instead, what she offered was a timeless acknowledgment of the passion between them.

Minutes ago, they might have had a verbal parry and thrust, but this was as honest as it got. Lizzie—Elizabeth—was as interested in him as he was in her. She hadn't run when she saw his implements of pleasure and pain, even though she lacked the courage to admit her curiosity.

There was something here. Something neither of them dared do anything about.

If he didn't have morals, he'd close the door behind him, lock it, then strip her down. She'd let him, too. The sexual hunger in the air told him that.

He'd wrap her wrists with his red tie and then secure her to the clothes bar above them. After he'd aroused her, he'd spank her ass and fuck her hard from behind. He'd take everything she offered and even some she didn't.

At the end of it all, when he released her, she would have no doubt who owned her, and the only sound from her mouth would be her gratitude.

But damn it all, he cared about what she thought of him. He couldn't fuck her and send her on her way like he did countless others.

Lizzie Ryan deserved to be treated like the princess her mother believed her to be. And by God, he would do that.

Even though, right this moment, he would rather die instead.

The dress wasn't for Braden. *How many times have I told myself that?*

Lizzie reminded herself that she was attending the event as hired help and nothing more. And she had three or four garments in her closet that were suitable for this evening's party.

No doubt she would have pulled something off a hanger and thrown it on as she left her house—except for the fact that the world's most annoying billionaire, Braden Gallagher, had lit up her entire world yesterday.

It had been years since she saw him, and her reaction to him had shattered her.

In her late teens, on the cusp of womanhood, she'd had a crush on the older, more sophisticated boy. What girl wouldn't? Especially one who came from a much poorer background.

Braden had it all. He was gorgeous, came from a perfect family, had a beautiful home where everything—air-conditioning, even heating—worked perfectly at the flip of a switch. Every part of his life was charmed. Not only did he get good grades, he was the captain of the football team. It seemed he had a different girlfriend almost every week. And numerous colleges sent him coveted acceptance letters.

As if that hadn't been enough to capture her schoolgirl fantasies, he was kind to her. She didn't see him much, mostly because he wasn't at his home when she was there with her mom. After school, Lizzie's aunt would sometimes drop her off at the Gallaghers' house. Once Lizzie finished her homework, she helped cook dinner. If he didn't have a game or practice, he'd hang out in the kitchen too.

One time, he'd arrived home from graduate school while she was showing off her prom dress for her mom.

She'd been embarrassed when he came in with a couple of

friends, but he'd told her how pretty she was and how lucky her date was.

He and his friends had grabbed water and sports drinks from the refrigerator before heading out to the pool, but he'd stopped at the door, looked back over his shoulder, and smiled at her.

Lizzie had almost swooned. His words, quick as they were, gave her more confidence than she'd known in her entire eighteen years.

Even though she now had a degree of her own and a successful career, she was shocked to discover he still held enormous power over her.

Having him find her in his closet had been humiliating. If she were smarter, she would have pushed past him and escaped back down the stairs.

Instead, she stayed, every part of her wanting to be near him, soaking up his attention.

Braden was impossibly tall, so much broader than she remembered. And he was unbelievably fit, without an ounce of fat anywhere. His dark hair was a bit on the long side, making him appear rakish. But it was his eyes that startled her. They were a grayish color, not quite green but not really blue. They were more like steel when it glinted in the sun.

Power cloaked him, and he wore it with as much ease as he did his tailored suit.

He was right, also, when he accused her of snooping.

She had been, and her lie had been brazen, and of course he'd seen right through it. While she had no real-world experience with the things in his third drawer, she was curious. A few of her friends were into it, and the ones who were married seemed to have authentic and deeply connected relationships. But she'd never met anyone she was interested in trying it with.

If Braden had arrived a few seconds before he did, he

might have found her tracing her fingers over the skeins of silky white rope.

That hadn't been what kept her awake for most of the night. His kiss had done that.

His fury at her words had left her reeling. She'd been reminding them both of her station in life, as well as seizing on any excuse to get away from him. The more she talked, the angrier he'd gotten. The first demanding moments when he'd held her tight had thrown her world out of its neatly structured orbit, and she hadn't known how to react. No man had ever been that physical with her before.

Lizzie's father had abandoned her mother while she was still pregnant. Because she'd seen how hard Eileen worked to make their lives better, Lizzie had kept herself focused on school, then work. She hadn't avoided men intentionally. Rather, she refused to let herself fall into emotional traps. Her girlfriends did plenty of crying over boys who hurt them, and some of them continued to do so. Lizzie was different. She was looking for a commitment. Love wasn't enough for her. She wanted a man who was steady and would respect their wedding vows. Eventually she wanted children, and she expected her husband to be an engaged father. And she let her dates know that early on.

Which made her behavior with Braden unfathomable.

He was the absolute last man on the planet she should kiss.

Behind his back, he was called the Scandalous Billionaire for a reason. He was often featured on gossip blogs, paired with different women. Rumors swirled about his liaisons, and once, he and a female companion had been caught in a compromising situation as his limousine had arrived for a massive Mardi Gras party on Galveston's Pier 21. Unexpectedly, a hired greeter had opened the back door before Braden and his companion were ready. Though they brazened it out, pretending nothing had happened, there were pictures, fortunately blurry enough for the couple to deny that it was them in the photo.

If Lizzie was going to choose someone to break all of her self-imposed rules with, she should select someone who wasn't a cad.

Unfortunately, last night he'd curled her toes as no one else ever had.

"Girl! What are you doing in there? I want to see the dress!" Crystal, her friend, pounded on the door, no doubt annoying the hell out of the very professional sales associates at one of Houston's exclusive boutiques at the shopping mecca known as the Galleria.

Stalling, once again lying to herself that she wasn't trying to impress Braden, Lizzie spun a slow, critical circle in the dressing room mirror.

The little black gown was stunning. The material fit her hips tightly, and the back had a slight V cutout. With its capped sleeves, the dress was simultaneously enticing and sedate.

"I mean it! Open up, Lizzie!" Crystal began knocking again, with every bit as much power as before.

"Okay, okay!" With a quick twist of her wrist, Lizzie unlocked the door.

"Girl!" Crystal exclaimed.

"Does that mean you like it?"

"Damn right I do."

The dress was shorter than Lizzie normally chose, and she tugged down slightly on the hem.

"Don't you dare do that. Show off them legs. That's why you drag me to sweaty yoga three days a week."

Actually, Lizzie went mainly to quiet her mind so she could escape the stress of her demanding job. The physical results were a bonus. "It's hot yoga."

"You call it anything you want. After five minutes, there's even underboob sweat. And I swear you're a masochist. The Painmaker is brutal."

Her physical trainer wasn't exactly a pain maker, but close enough. At first, she and Crystal had gone together. Then one time, while doing a pushup, Crystal collapsed into a heap on the mat and announced she was never doing that again. She went to the locker room and never walked through the door of the fitness center ever again.

"Look at yourself. You totally rock that dress."

Lizzy wrinkled her nose. Even though she worked out, her body wasn't close to perfect, but the cut of the dress accented all her positive attributes and downplayed the ones she was most critical of. The dress was meant for her.

"Are you going to buy it?"

The saleswoman breezed in and bubbled over with effusive compliments. Crystal rolled her eyes and propped a hand on her hip.

For a third time, Lizzie looked at the price tag. Really, she should wear something already hanging in her closet. But after yoga and a quick shower followed by a trip to the coffeeshop, Crystal suggested they go shopping—not that either of them needed an excuse.

"You know what they say," Crystal started. "Don't look at the amount. Figure out how many times you're going to it wear it, and calculate the cost that way. So, if you go to another five parties, the dress is…" She shrugged. "I don't know. I suck at math. But it's practically free."

"You're no help." Not once had her friend tried to talk Lizzie out of buying something. Crystal was a world-class instigator, seeming to get as much pleasure out of Lizzie's purchases as she did herself.

"But you dress up all the time."

She did. Lizzie worked for the Sterling brand of hotels,

and she worked on opening new properties for the chain. As part of her job, she attended numerous events where they hosted exclusive parties for event and wedding planners. They also did soft openings for the bars and restaurants, and those were also upscale. At the beginning of a job, she'd be in a hardhat. By the time she was ready to wrap it up, she was in tall heels and gowns.

"I'm telling you this." Crystal leaned forward, going for the kill. "If I wanted to do the dirty with Braden Gallagher, I'd buy it."

Lizzie gasped. "I don't want to sleep with him!"

"Uh-huh."

*Okay.* So maybe she did.

Wrinkling her nose, she gave herself one last critical stare.

"You're getting it, aren't you?" Crystal whooped.

Nerves skidded through her tummy. "Yes." There were a dozen reasons she shouldn't. Braden Gallagher was dangerous. His kiss had been possessive—frighteningly so. And while he'd held her close, his erection pressed against her. He wanted her, and she wanted him.

For the first time in her life, Lizzy was feeling reckless.

## CHAPTER TWO

"You look absolutely fucking gorgeous."

Lizzie froze as Braden captured her wrist. Then gently he drew her away from the party, behind a potted palm where they'd be safe from the glare of the lights and prying eyes.

Lost in his gaze, she couldn't breathe.

Everything except Braden disappeared. The music spilling from inside the house and voices from the party-goers on the pool deck fell silent, replaced by the sound of her rushing heartbeat.

"I've been waiting all evening for a chance to be alone with you."

As Lizzie dressed and applied her makeup earlier in the evening, she'd been hoping for this reaction. And yet... Just like yesterday, being the focus of Braden's attention overwhelmed her. "We shouldn't do this."

"Do what?"

"Whatever it is you're thinking." She was fairly certain she knew exactly what was going through his mind. "Dinner will be served in a little while, and there are things I need to take care of." Though his mother had hired an official event planner, Lizzie was helping out, and there were myriad last-minute details that still needed to be handled.

"You're wearing that dress for me."

She gasped, hoping to hide her reaction. How had he seen through her so effortlessly? "I did not."

"You most certainly did." His grin was slow and confident. "And I'm glad. I've been thinking about kissing you since the moment I first saw you tonight."

Though she'd never admit it, that idea consumed her as well.

Because she knew parking would be at a premium, she'd decided to use a car service rather than driving herself. Braden had waved off the attendants hired for the evening and strode over to help her from the vehicle, as if she were one of the guests.

He'd stolen her breath.

Yesterday, in a suit, he was handsome. Today, in a tuxedo, he was devastating. There were any number of beautiful socialites at the event, but he only had eyes for her.

He leaned a little closer to her.

"Braden…"

"You're a siren, sent to tempt me."

Why her? Because she was off-limits?

"Kiss me, Lizzie."

This time, he was asking. There was no anger behind it, and he wanted her to be the one to initiate it. The truth was, she had no idea what she was supposed to do. "I've never… I mean…"

*"Fuck."* His voice was hoarse, gruff, maybe from anticipation or need. Regardless, it stirred an undeniable response in her.

Lizzie was wearing her highest heels, and she still had to lift up to brush her lips against his.

"What do I smell? Perfume?"

She didn't normally wear any, but today she'd selected something light, with the faintest hint of honeysuckle, and she'd dabbed a little on her pulse points. "Yes."

"I like it. Put your arms around my neck." Instead of waiting for her to follow his instruction, he gently took hold of her and guided her into place. "Better?"

"Yes." Again, with more confidence, she gave him another gentle kiss.

"Woman, your beautiful innocence might be the death of me."

Unsurprisingly Braden then took control. He kissed her, but in a totally different way than he had last night. This time, he was gentle, coaxing a response rather than insisting on one.

She tasted something strong and masculine on him, perhaps whiskey.

As the seconds passed, she relaxed into him, and he pressed one hand against her back and tucked the other into her hair. When he invited her closer, she went. His groan of appreciation reverberated through her, daring her to be bolder, and she opened her mouth wider.

He pulled back long enough to meet her gaze, then seized her mouth again.

Was this how he made love? As if it was the only thing that mattered?

But what about the things she'd seen in his closet? She shuddered, imagining him wrapping her in that white rope and trailing the soft strands of the flogger over her body. From yesterday, she knew he wasn't always gentle, but even then, he'd never lost control. So he might do more than caress her with the strips of leather.

Heat pooled through her. Who was this newer, more

reckless Lizzie? She was seconds away from reaching for his tie and plucking the ends loose.

She was grateful when he ended the kiss and reached back to unlink her arms.

"We have to stop right this moment. Otherwise we're leaving the party and never coming back."

He was being rational. Thank God he was capable of it, because she wasn't sure that she was.

With his thumbnail, Braden traced her swollen mouth. There was a tiny fairy light behind them, enough for her to see a glint from his ring. She glanced at the piece of jewelry, expecting to see his college insignia on it. Instead there was an owl on it, with tiny emeralds for eyes. Before she could ask about it, Braden spoke again.

"Don't freshen up your lipstick. When I look at you for the rest of the night, I want to know I was the one who did it to you."

Because she didn't know what to say, she ran a hand across the front of her dress, then unconsciously tugged at the hem.

"I don't want to get back. But people will be wondering where we are."

His words were a splash of reality in her face.

This interlude had been stupid. What if someone had noticed him stealing her away from the party? His reputation would be fine. After all, his conquests were legendary. But she didn't want to be whispered about.

He looked around the enormous plant, then glanced back at her. "It's safe. You can go. I'll follow in about thirty seconds."

Suspecting she'd gone a little mad since yesterday, she tore her gaze away from his, then double-checked that there was no one around before stepping out and making a beeline toward the house.

"Elizabeth?"

She'd almost made it across the concrete patio when a familiar voice stopped her. *Rafe?* Her heart somewhere in the vicinity of her knees, she turned to her boss.

Rafe Sterling owned thousands of hotels worldwide, and she was fortunate to work for him. She'd only been able to afford to attend a community college, but she'd worked damn hard to earn good grades, and she'd won a scholarship to Houston's biggest university.

A few years ago, his company founded the hospitality school that she'd attended. Students ran the Sterling University Hotel, as well as the restaurants and coffee shop there. It afforded an unusual learning experience. In her years there, she'd served in every position, from waitstaff, to housekeeping, to barista, cashier, to front desk clerk. She'd even been a bellhop and concierge. She'd particularly enjoyed her stint as a valet because she'd had the opportunity to drive both a Ferrari and a Lamborghini.

During the last year of her studies, she'd moved into management of various departments. And because she was at the top of her class, for the final months, she'd served as the hotel's general manager.

Rafe himself had stayed there and had met with her.

After graduation, he'd offered her a job.

She'd spent a year abroad serving an externship of sorts, learning more about his business model and honing her customer service skills.

When she returned, Rafe approached her about moving into her current position. He'd told her it would be terribly demanding and cut her social life into tiny ribbons. But because of her experience in every facet of his operations, she was perfect for the job. It was only later that she learned that his other openers had fifteen to twenty years of on-the-job training.

Still, it was perfect for her. Houston was home. Since her next posting could take her anywhere in the world, she was determined to enjoy as much time as she could with her friends and family members. "Mr. Sterling! How nice to see you."

"Rafe," he corrected, as always. "Please." He shook her hand. "The Gallaghers and Sterlings have been friends for years."

That shouldn't have surprised her. Both families were from old money, and no doubt they shared a social circle.

"I didn't expect to see you here."

She would never be included on the guest list. At the moment, she was so far out of her depth that she wanted the world to swallow her whole. "My mother has been the housekeeper here for almost twenty-five years." From the time she discovered she was pregnant with Lizzie, scared and alone. Lizzie shouldn't be embarrassed in front of her boss, but unaccountably she was. "I'm here to help out."

"They're lucky to have you."

As always, Rafe Sterling was a gentleman, and she was grateful. "Is Hope with you?" She was referring to his fiancée, the renowned Houston matchmaker. Not only was Hope a strategic businesswoman responsible for a number of recent, high-profile weddings; she was as gorgeous as she was lovely. Having her here would ease the awkwardness.

"No. Unfortunately she's traveling."

"Will you give her my regards?" To make a getaway, she switched back to a role she knew well—hospitality. "May I offer you a glass of champagne? There's also a full bar with your favorite whiskey."

"I've kept you long enough. I apologize."

"Ah, Rafe!"

Even though he was behind her, Braden's deep, sensual voice drizzled down her spine. "Enjoy your evening," she said to her boss. She started to walk away, but Braden was there, momentarily touching her back while taking his place beside her.

"How are you?" The two men shook hands. In the reflection of the light, she realized that Rafe also had an owl on his ring. "I see you've met Lizzie."

"I've known Elizabeth for some time. In fact, she's one of Sterling's greatest assets."

"Oh?" Braden asked as he lowered his hand.

"She's one of my openers." When Braden didn't respond, Rafe went on with an explanation. "Every time we open a new property, I assign someone to oversee every aspect—sales, food and beverage, training, customer service, amenities, IT, that sort of thing. Of course, each department has its own manager, but they all report to that one key person until I bring on an operations director. The opener stays on the job through the first few weeks to ensure a smooth transition. It's a relatively new position, and we've found it adds a layer of continuity that was sometimes missing."

"Impressive. I had no idea." Braden placed his hand on her again, this time in the spot where the dress plunged into the deep V. His touch was as intimate as it was proprietorial. Turning toward her, he went on. "You know how to run every department in the hotel and take care of all the details that go into the grand opening?"

Uncomfortable at being the center of attention, as well as with the way her body was responding to Braden with a rush of pheromones, she shrugged. "Mr. Sterling is generous. His training program was comprehensive."

"As you might imagine, I don't hire from the outside for this position. I recruit from the top one percent of my team."

"Aren't you afraid someone will steal her away?"

What the hell kind of question was that? And how was Rafe supposed to answer it? In silent warning, she unobtrusively placed her stiletto on Braden's foot. If he continued, she wouldn't hesitate to bring him to his knees.

"Am I afraid someone will steal her away? Every damn day." With an eyebrow raised, Rafe considered Braden. "Should I be?"

Suddenly this was beyond absurd. "Gentlemen, Sterling Worldwide has my complete loyalty. I intend to be there as long as they will have me. If you'll excuse me?"

Lizzie escaped Braden's heated touch and hurried inside of the house, where she paused for a second to collect herself. She took a steadying breath and reminded herself she was a professional businesswoman, and she was here tonight as part of the staff.

Her mother was frowning. Obviously, from her vantage point behind the kitchen island, she'd seen the entire exchange. *Damn.*

"What is it?" Lizzie asked.

"They're both still watching you."

Every one of Lizzie's impulses demanded that she look over her shoulder, and it took all of her self-control not to.

"What is all that about?" Eileen asked.

"I honestly have no idea." Lizzie shook her head. Braden Gallagher had acted possessive of her, in front of her boss, which was absurd. She and Braden had shared a kiss or two, hardly enough for him to feel as if he had the right to behave that way. "What can I help with?" She diverted her mother back to party responsibilities, which was Lizzie's best way out of the conversation. After all, there was no way she was going to confess that she'd behaved badly with Braden a few minutes ago.

One of the bartenders popped her head inside the room. "We need more champagne."

Lizzie seized the opportunity to escape. "I'll handle it."

"Do you know where it is?" Eileen pointed toward the farthest end of the house. "In the study."

*Interesting.* That was one of the few rooms in the house that she'd never been in. Though her mother dusted and swept the room periodically, Braden reportedly never used it. The space had been designed by his grandfather and then occupied by his father, but Braden had opted to have an office upstairs.

At the end of the hallway, Lizzie turned the handle and pushed the door open. No wonder he didn't come in here. With its oak paneling and heavy leather furniture and a Tiffany lamp, it was all but a shrine to a bygone era. Trophies lined built-in shelves. College pennants and Greek symbols were tacked up. Framed pictures were hung from the walls.

Though she should grab a few bottles of champagne from the refrigerator that had been temporarily installed in the room, she couldn't resist a closer look at the black-and-white photographs. She recognized Braden's grandfather shaking hands with a man who'd been the president of the United States. In another he was standing next to an astronaut.

She glanced around, taking in the rest of the photos, some featuring Braden's father. There were a number of people she didn't recognize in the shots, but more than a few that she did. Actors, performers, politicians, scientists.

On the oversize and intricately carved desk, there was an owl with emerald eyes, flanked by laurel leaves—a much larger replica of the one on Braden's ring.

Intrigued, she returned to the photo of Braden's grandfather shaking hands with the president.

Both of their rings bore the same owl.

She glanced around again, taking in the lowercase Greek *Z* on a banner. What in the world? Some sort of fraternity? It was another reminder of how little she knew about the man who'd kissed her.

From outside, the sound of laughter reached her, jolting her back to reality.

Quickly, she grabbed half a dozen bottles of champagne, loaded them into a box, then hurried back to the kitchen, where she gave them to the party planner, who'd been on her way to find out what was keeping Lizzie.

Eileen frowned at her.

"I was being nosy. Is Braden in a fraternity?"

"Of a sort." Eileen turned on the faucet and began rinsing dishes.

*Odd.* Her mother wasn't generally evasive, which heightened Lizzie's curiosity. "Along with the president of the United States?" Maybe it was a college thing. No doubt all the Gallagher men had attended the same one.

"Hmm."

"Mom?"

"If you want to know anything more, you will have to ask Braden." With that, Eileen returned to work.

Waitstaff began letting guests know that dinner was being served in the tents. Afterward, there would be announcements and a toast celebrating Mr. and Mrs. Gallagher's anniversary. Cake and coffee would follow, and at the same time, the quartet would begin playing in the ballroom.

Because they had a short break, Lizzie and her mother ate a small meal in the kitchen. Eileen steered the conversation toward their own family.

"Will you be there tomorrow night?"

Lizzie's aunt Virginia had married into a large Latino family, and she'd enthusiastically embraced the culture. Now every Sunday, Virginia made dinner for anyone who wanted to come over. Recently, one of her sons had started distilling his own tequila, and each time he came, he brought a bottle or two. The gathering was now known as the Triple T—tamales, tacos, and tequila. Some weeks only a few people showed up, but at times, there were as many as thirty attendees.

"Sandra is bringing the baby."

"Then I'll definitely be there." Lizzie grinned. She hadn't gotten to meet her cousin's newborn, and she was looking forward to snuggling the little bundle of joy.

Their conversation was interrupted by the party planner entering the house. "Do you mind letting the band know it's time for them to start?"

"Happy to." After snatching a mint from a bowl on the counter, Lizzie went into the ballroom and chatted with the band, making sure that they had beverages. Then she double-checked that the two people behind the small makeshift bar were all set.

"We may need some more bottled water. It's pretty hot tonight."

"Good idea."

A half hour later, as more and more people drifted inside, the atmosphere around her became supercharged. *Braden.* Even without seeing him or hearing him speak, she knew he was there.

"Dance with me?"

His deep and rich voice slid over her, awakening an immediate response in her. Despite her best efforts to avoid him, he'd found her, making her wonder if he'd been looking for her.

Lizzie turned to face him, all the while looking for an excuse to escape. A few couples were already swaying to an old Frank Sinatra song. The bartender in the corner was mixing a drink. Everything was under control. "I was just going to check on..." *What?* The idea of being in his arms again made rational thought vanish. In a rushed whisper, she finished her sentence. "Something."

"I'm sure you won't be missed for the next three minutes."

How could he not understand her position? "I can't." She couldn't, no matter how much she wanted to. "The host doesn't fraternize with the help."

"Fraternize, is it?" A smile played around his mouth.

Since he'd found her in his closet, he'd been gruff, serious, and enticingly sexy. But this softer side of him was irresistible. "People will talk."

"I don't spend a lot of time concerned about that."

"You might not. But I do." Her mom would have questions, and perhaps his mother as well.

He shrugged. "You're the help. Do I understand that correctly? So in this instance, it makes me your boss?"

"Don't." She saw where he was going. "That's sneaky, using my words against me." The billionaire was as determined as he was clever.

"It's only a dance." His voice was persuasive. "In front of all these people." He waved his hand, then leaned in a little closer. "It's not an all-out attempt at seduction."

*Oh, but it is.* And it was working.

"There are only about two minutes left in the song. What harm could there be?"

To her? A lot. She wasn't a woman capable of switching her emotions on and off.

"We can do it here. Away from prying eyes."

"Braden."

"Say yes."

Without giving her time to protest, he wrapped his arms around her, claiming her the moment she agreed.

Braden held her tight, as if he never wanted to let her go. At first, she held her body rigid, but he was a force of nature, and she was powerless to resist him.

"We fit together nice."

He was right, but for the sake of her sanity, she couldn't agree.

"Makes me wonder what else would be perfect between us."

For a moment, no one else existed, and she realized why so many women fell for him. She'd been tempting fate when she bought this dress, swiped on the lipstick, and dabbed on the drops of fragrance.

His grip was light, and for one tantalizing minute, she wondered what it might be like if she were his social equal, if he was interested in her as a woman. Since both thoughts were ludicrous, she shooed them away.

She had found success in her life because she didn't allow men to distract her. Lizzie told herself to remember that.

When the song ended, she pulled back, desperate to get away. "Thank you." She forced a polite smile as she reminded herself that it had only been yesterday that she'd found his tie under the couch in the living room.

This billionaire was a complete scoundrel. And Elizabeth Ryan was too smart to become another in his long line of conquests.

&

"You should stay."

Shocked, Lizzie turned. Braden's shoulders were propped on one of the thick sliding-glass partitions that had recently been closed.

Outside, a few torches still flickered, and the fairy lights danced in the gentle breeze. The party had ended almost an hour ago, but it had taken that long for the caterers to clean up and for her and her mother to put the kitchen to rights again.

Lizzie had walked her mother to her car before returning for her cell phone to request a car.

It *had* been a long night. Her feet throbbed, and she

longed to slip out of her heels. At the very least, she should have brought a second pair of shoes to change into. But when she left the house, she'd been thinking about what would complement the dress...and about the way her calves would look in them.

"I mean it. There's no need to leave."

His suggestion was ludicrous, and she needed to refuse right away.

"It's late." He glanced at the massive clock on the kitchen wall and winced. "Or early, depending on your point of view."

All the more reason for her to leave now.

"You've been working hard on this event for at least two days. I've got a soaker tub you might enjoy."

Her rented home was small and only had a shower in the master suite, and there were times she missed taking a long bath. But she wasn't an idiot. She knew there was only one soaker tub in his house. And that was in the master suite.

"I have plenty of guest rooms." He grinned. "Not really sure how many."

"Eight." She knew; after all, there'd been many times she'd helped her mother change the sheets on all of the beds.

"I give you my word as a gentleman that I'll behave." He raised his right hand.

That was the biggest part of this whole problem. Part of her didn't want him to keep his distance. She wanted to be ravaged by him, swept away for once in her life.

"You can be asleep before you'd even arrive home—well, depending on where you live in the city."

After their dance earlier, she'd done her best to avoid Braden. That wasn't easy, though. All of her instincts were attuned to him. If he came within fifty feet of her, tiny goose bumps chased down her arms. She could pick out the timbre of his baritone voice in a roomful of men.

Now, he was even more enticing. He'd discarded his jacket and unknotted his bow tie, leaving the ends dangling starkly against his crisp white shirt. The look was every bit as sexy as she'd earlier imagined it might be.

"What do you say?"

Survival instinct screamed no. But instead, she exhaled a shaky breath and gave him a wobbly grin. "You had me at soaker tub."

CHAPTER THREE

Spending the night at Braden's house was not one of Lizzie's smartest decisions.

She'd been soaking in the tub with her head tipped back and her eyes closed, luxuriating in the magnificence of the moment, until she heard him moving about in his bedroom, and his closet.

Because she was afraid of seeing him naked, she lowered herself a little, until her shoulders were under the water, and she stayed that way for far too long. Finally, when the water chilled enough to make her teeth chatter, she stepped out, then dried off with one of his big fluffy towels. Then she slipped into a T-shirt that he'd given her. The hem came to midthigh, and she told herself it wasn't skimpy. After all, it covered more of her than her dress had.

His shirt smelled like him, even though that was impossible. It had been folded on a shelf, fresh from the laundry. But to her it was snuggly and warm, and it held a slight scent of spice.

When she emerged from the bathroom, he was nowhere to be found. She rolled her eyes heavenward in a little show of gratitude. Then she chided herself for hiding out in the first place. If she'd been a little braver, she could have already been in bed.

After another quick glance around, she dashed toward the bedroom she'd selected. It was on the opposite side of the house, as far away from Braden as she could get. Once the door clicked closed, she hurried to the bed, where she yanked the covers up to her chin and listened for sounds of him. The air conditioner kicked on, and its whisper was enough to make any other sound impossible to discern.

A few minutes later, she turned over and closed her eyes, only to pop them open almost right away.

Telling herself to stop being ridiculous, that Braden wasn't standing there waiting to take advantage of her, she drew a steadying breath and tried again. Each time she started to drift off to sleep, memories of their time together rushed through her mind, one after the other, each vivid in color and emotion. She replayed the scene in his closet, then the one where he'd pulled her behind a palm. His kisses, from intense to promising, had each been stimulating, and they'd evoked unique responses in her.

And there were the toys she'd found in his bedroom...

Until yesterday, she'd never had much of a desire to experiment sexually. But now, she pictured herself tied for his pleasure, maybe even blindfolded. Shocking her, she even wondered what she might look like with his gag in her mouth.

There was no way she was going to be able to sleep as long as they were both under the same roof. With his gorgeous smile and devastating intent, Braden Gallagher had started to dismantle every defense she'd erected to keep herself safe.

In frustration, she tossed and turned for over an hour,

unable to get comfortable, despite punching the pillow into numerous different shapes.

Sometime after three, she gave up and climbed out of bed. She tiptoed to the door, then opened it a crack. The lights were out, and the house was quiet.

Holding her breath, just in case, Lizzie crept down the cool marble stairs and padded into the kitchen.

Because she'd spent countless hours here after school released for the day, this place was comfortable.

Wondering if her mother still kept a pile of homemade chocolate chip cookies stashed away, Lizzie rooted through the pantry. *"Yes,"* she whispered as she triumphantly pulled out a canister.

She carried it to the island then took a glass from a cupboard shelf and placed it on the counter before grabbing a carton of milk from the refrigerator.

"Is there enough for two?"

Lizzie screamed and jumped, nearly dropping the half-gallon container. How had she not heard him?

Shaking from the fright he'd given her, she spun.

When she saw him, her eyes widened, and she couldn't find her voice.

He lazed in the doorjamb, wearing only a pair of boxer briefs. The tight material hugged his hips, and the front pouch showed off his semierect cock.

Stunned, heated, she clutched the carton to her chest.

"Sorry. I didn't mean to startle you." His voice was rich and sleep roughened, dragging across her senses like diamonds on steel. "Couldn't settle?"

"That sometimes happens when I'm not in my own bed." It was a total lie, and every one of her nerve endings was twisted inside out.

His jaw was unshaven, making him seem sexier than ever. Unable to stop herself, she looked at him, appreciating his broad shoulders and honed chest that had a sexy smattering of hair.

Lizzie told herself to affect an air of nonchalance, pretending she often found herself alone with an ultrahot alpha male in his kitchen in the middle of the night.

Right now, she didn't know how to stop herself from letting her gaze wander lower, to his tight abdomen. He had a workout room in the house, and there was no doubt he used it.

His legs were lean and muscular, probably from cycling or running.

Then, damn it, she was unable to resist temptation to once again look at his pelvis. Arousal flashed through her in a wave of hunger she'd never experienced before. It was as frightening as it was irresistible.

He was regarding her, and if his lazy smile was anything to go by, he didn't mind the way she'd been staring at him.

To distract herself from the unwelcome sensations zipping through her, Lizzie carried the milk to the island.

"Are you going to be selfish with the cookies? I'll tell your mom you wouldn't share."

Because his comment was so lighthearted and absurd—a contradiction to his potent masculinity—she gave a small laugh.

Without waiting for another response, he pushed away from the door. Within seconds, he'd pulled back a stool from the island and took a seat.

Lizzie contemplated fleeing back to her room, but now that he was up, she knew she wouldn't be able to go to sleep anyway.

She transferred a pile of cookies onto a plate then slid it in front of him. "Milk also?"

"I haven't done this in years."

Neither had she. "I'll take that as a yes?"

"Please." He nodded.

After she took down a second glass and filled each of them, then returned the carton to the fridge, the situation became even more awkward, at least for her. He seemed completely at ease.

"Thank you." He lifted his glass and tipped it toward her in a slight toast. Then, surprising her, he dunked his cookie in the milk.

For a moment, he looked more carefree than she ever remembered. Ever since she met him, he'd been serious, maybe to the point of somber. Or maybe this was an act, part of his effort to charm her. If so, it was working.

"I always appreciated the way your mom had treats for me."

She took a drink and propped her hips against the sink, about as far away from his as possible.

"After little Mandy…"

Intrigued, she waited. Her mother almost never spoke of Braden's baby sister, who'd been born premature and passed a few weeks later.

"Things changed." He finished his treat, and she wondered if he'd go on or whether that was as much as he intended to share.

"Mom used to be happy. And then, all the joy was sucked from our lives."

Lizzie had heard that his parents separated shortly after that. Even now they lived in different homes, even though they'd never filed for divorce.

"They lost a child. And I lost my little sister and my parents." He shrugged, but there was pain in his eyes, making it difficult for her to breathe. "There was a year or more of this horrible, unnatural silence. No television, no music. When I look back, I'm sure my mother was depressed."

He couldn't have been more than eight or nine at the

time, not nearly old enough to understand what was happening.

"And then came the yelling. Well, not from Mom, never from her, but from Dad. The louder he was, the more she cried. It didn't get any better when he left. In fact, it might have been worse. Grief takes its toll."

"Oh, Braden. I'm so sorry. I really had no idea." While she'd heard the story before, she'd been removed from it. She was never at the house without her mother, and Eileen spread joy wherever she went.

"Without your mom…" He shrugged. "Having her here made things bearable."

More than ever, she understood the offense she'd caused yesterday when she suggested her mother might lose her job. He was sincere about how much Eileen meant to him.

"I didn't mean to be melancholy." He snatched up another cookie. "Where does she hide them?"

"It's a secret. You didn't even know they were there, and if I tell you, you'll eat them all, and then I won't have any when I come over."

"So you really *weren't* going to share?"

"Nope." She took a great big bite. "Not at all."

They exchanged goofy grins. Once they faded, the atmosphere ignited.

"Lizzie…"

Even though she should resist him, she wanted him with a ferocity that wouldn't be denied.

Each motion purposeful, he slipped from the stool and strode toward her.

"Those things in your drawers?" She faltered, unable to express herself. Why had she even mentioned her fears?

Braden captured her shoulders in a touch that was unbelievably light and reassuring. "Yes?" he asked.

"They're terrifying."

"They don't need to be. Everything I own can be sensual and nothing more. It depends on how the toy is used. And I want to be clear about this—I have no expectations of you. We don't have to use any of them."

Once again, unbidden, her thoughts turned to the rope she'd fondled, the gag she'd seen.

"Was there anything that interested you?"

"No."

"Lizzie, Lizzie." He trailed a finger down the side of her jaw. "You'd make a terrible poker player. When you're not being truthful, you speak more quickly than normal. It's slight. But noticeable because I'm watching every little thing you do, listening to each word you utter."

"That's ridiculous." It wasn't. She'd all but snapped the words.

"Is it? You did it when we were in my closet and I asked if you'd opened the third drawer. And again, a few minutes ago when you said you couldn't sleep because you were in a strange bed."

Had anyone ever seen through her as well as he did? That idea was even more frightening than his BDSM proclivities.

"We can try anything you want, or nothing at all."

She nodded.

"I want to make love to you, Lizzie."

That word. She would have preferred he say *fuck*, something that would allow her to build an emotional barrier between them. There was no doubt he was far more casual about sex than she was, so everything he did had to be purposeful, as a way to build intimacy. For her, it was working.

"I have condoms, and we'll use them."

She squeezed her eyes shut as she surrendered to the inevitable.

"Don't hide from me."

That was exactly what she wanted to do. "It'd be easier for me," she admitted when she looked at him again.

"Maybe it would." He rested his thumb against the hollow of her throat. "But this isn't something that's simply going to happen to you. It's something we're doing together. That's the magic of it. And watching your reactions matters to me, especially the first time we're together."

*First time.* His words indicated he anticipated this would happen more than once, and that seemed at odds with what she knew about him.

"I'm going to take off your T-shirt."

She glanced around. No blinds covered the glass.

"There aren't any neighbors close enough to see anything."

The few times she'd been with a man, she undressed in the dark. But she didn't protest when he caught the hem of the T-shirt and drew it up her thighs.

His touch was sure as he continued, exposing skin, a fraction of an inch at a time.

"So beautiful."

He was a master with his approving tone.

Braden continued, until he bared her breasts. In the chilly room, her nipples pebbled, and he scraped his nails across them lightly, making her breath catch.

"Perfect. You're perfect, Lizzie."

She raised her arms as he finished removing the shirt. Still looking at her, he tossed the garment in the direction of the countertop before stripping off her panties.

Fighting off the instinctive desire to cover herself, she stood there, nerves slamming into her in waves.

"I've thought of this moment."

So had she. But in her fantasies, she'd been much more confident.

"You're even more exquisite than I imagined."

His words not only soothed her, they emboldened her.

Braden cradled her breasts, then tweaked her nipples. She gasped from the pleasure that surged through her.

"You're sensitive?" he asked.

"Very much so."

"In that case, I'll be gentle with you."

"Don't." *Please.* Lizzie had never been bold when it came to asking for what she wanted in the bedroom, but Braden seemed to expect it. "I liked it."

"Did you? And this? Tell me if you like this." His eyes darkened before he lowered his head to lick one of the beaded tips.

She jerked, then froze. "It's…"

"Tell me."

How could she describe something she'd never experienced before? "I feel as though I'm vibrating on the inside."

"That's good?"

"It's indescribable."

"And how's this?" He sucked on her nipple and slowly increased the pressure until she moaned.

Immediately he backed off again. She sighed with impatience.

"So that was pleasure, rather than pain?"

"It was both." *I think.* She couldn't separate one from the other. All she knew was that she liked it.

"So you want more? For me to push you a little further?"

"Yes."

Braden started again but this time, when she whimpered, he continued. Her responses overwhelmed her, and she curled her fingers into his shoulders.

Unthinkingly she moved her hips toward him, and he continued to suck. Shocking her, he moved a hand between her legs to stroke her. Within seconds, an orgasm began to blossom.

"Are you going to come for me, Lizzie? So quickly?"

Her last partner had never given her this much attention. Once he ejaculated, he fell asleep. After a few weeks, she lost the little interest she'd had in sex, then, shortly after, the relationship itself.

"That's what I want. Come for me." He eased a finger inside her, then a second alongside it. He moved his hand slightly and pressed against her G-spot.

With a scream, she came, splintering, falling...

Moments later, she was wrapped in his arms, safe, secure. And she wasn't quite sure how she'd ended up there.

It took forever for Lizzie to regain her equilibrium. When she did, she flattened one of her palms against his chest and pushed back a few inches.

Braden was looking down at her, wearing a wide, silly grin, as if he was proud of himself.

No one had ever spent that much time focused on her satisfaction. It was unbelievably appealing. Lizzie gave herself a mental shake. She needed to be careful. After all, he'd earned his scandalous reputation, and she was nothing more than an addition to his long list of conquests.

But right this moment, she didn't feel that way. Instead, she felt special, and that was addictive.

"Shall we go upstairs?"

She had to know, even if she never saw him again after tonight. "Yes."

His smile faded, replaced by a flare of possession in his steely gray-blue eyes. Every part of her responded to him, making him potentially lethal to her well-being.

Right this moment, she was willing to sacrifice her emotions on the altar of his seduction.

CHAPTER FOUR

Lizzie's breath threatened to choke her. Once again, she was in his closet, in front of the open drawer. Though the rope intrigued her, she couldn't make herself reach for it.

"Anything you'd like to try?" His voice contained nothing but patient encouragement, giving her courage.

"The... Uhm..."

He waited.

Now that she was with Braden, she understood the allure of BDSM. He could offer her the world, and she was eager to experience it. "Can we start with the red tie?"

"Excellent choice. Please get it for us."

She'd expected him to press the button that would slide out the rack, but instead, he waited for her to do what he said. His first command?

A seductive mix of fear and excitement unfurled in her stomach.

Even though her finger trembled, she did what he said, then plucked the silky tie from its hook and offered it to him.

Instead of accepting it right away, he continued to look

down at her, overwhelming her. "Please extend your arms, then cross your wrists."

Mouth dry, she did so. Only then did he take the tie from her grip.

"Do you know what a safe word is?"

"I've heard the term." Standing before him, naked, talking about it as it referred to her—*them*—unnerved her.

His gaze was intense, and she couldn't look away. "Tell me what you know about it."

This conversation shouldn't be difficult. After all, they were going to be intimate in moments. "It's a word that I say if I'm..." What? She realized she knew so little about BDSM that she wasn't certain exactly when she might use a safe word. "Scared? Or if something hurts?"

"Yes." He nodded. "And more. If you use a safe word, our play will stop immediately."

*Play?* It didn't seem like it to her.

"For example..." He began to wrap her wrists.

The bond wasn't tight, and no doubt she could slip from it if she wanted.

He tugged it tighter. "Let's say we're doing something that you're into. But then you change your mind. Or something happens mentally, emotionally, or physically... Like you said, you might get scared. Or perhaps remember a bad experience. Or even get a cramp in your body. If your boundaries are pushed, you do not have to keep going. You will never be judged for it. In fact, I will be more upset if you try to push through. I don't want you harmed in any way."

This was far more complex and intriguing than she'd imagined.

"A lot of people use the word *red*. And some avoid stop or no. In a scene, the bottom might want to scream no or stop while the—"

"Bottom?"

"Ah. Sorry." He grinned. "A Top is the person who is in the more dominant position for the sake of the scene. The bottom is the person who is submitting. In some relationships, people can be switches, meaning they go back and forth between the roles."

This was new to her, and a little confusing. "I thought the terms were Dominant and submissive."

"They can be. But the words have meaning, and until you fully offer your submission, I prefer these terms."

"How utterly Dominant of you."

"It is, isn't it?" He quirked his eyebrows in a way that was adorable but also mind-blowingly sexy.

While she was staring at him, he yanked on the tie, and she gasped.

"Have you selected a word?"

"I'll go with red."

He tightened it a little more. "Say it."

"Now?"

"Yes."

"Red," she whispered, even though she didn't want to.

Instantly, he loosened her, setting her free and stroking the tiny marks he'd made. "That's how it always works. You have my word that I'll always care for you."

"Even if you're into it?" Why had she even asked that? His explanation had been explicit. "I mean, there are times, right…? Like during sex…"

"Your needs come before mine. It's my obligation as a Top to care for you."

The idea was new, and thrilling.

"Is there anything I need to know? Phobias? Things you absolutely wouldn't want to do?"

Her brain clouded over. "Honestly? I'm having trouble thinking."

"Then we'll discuss things as we go forward, as we grow

together in this relationship."

Now she was reeling.

"Blindfold?"

Realizing he was staring, waiting for an answer, she shook her head. "I'm sorry. I didn't hear." She had. She just wasn't able to process what he said.

"Are you willing to try a blindfold?"

A wave of trepidation washed over her. "I'd like to think about it."

"Being tied while I ravish you?" He grinned.

"Ravish?" What an antiquated, illicit way to put it.

"I intend to do precisely that."

*Yum.* "Being tied sounds interesting."

"Spanking?"

Her knees weakened, and he put a steadying hand beneath her elbow. "Maybe. I... Yes?" Images crashed into her. Being over his lap with her buttocks upturned. Or face-down on the bed with her hands secured and wearing a blindfold. "As long as it's not too painful. That scares me."

"You're important to me, sweet Lizzie. For me, the point of this is your pleasure."

Skepticism made her furrow her eyebrows. "Really?"

"Most definitely." Then he smiled in a slow, measured way that bound her to him in a way that ropes or ties could never do. "Don't misunderstand. Nothing excites me more than the idea of turning you on. Blowing your mind, even."

*Yes, please.* "That sounds like a tall order, Mr. Gallagher."

"You'll be the judge. You have your safe word. In time, you'll learn to trust me also."

Perhaps stupidly, she already did.

"Anything else you want to try?"

"I'm curious about... Uhm..."

"Talk to me," he encouraged. "We need honesty for this to work."

She had never been braver in her life than at this moment. "Maybe I will try a blindfold after all."

"Would you like to choose one?" He slid open his third drawer.

There were several nestled on crushed velvet. "Why do you have so many?"

"They're different. That one, for example, is bigger than the others and thicker as well. Total blackout. Others are made from different fabric, and they let in varying amounts of light. So it depends on the experience you want."

"I'm confused again. I thought the Dominant—or Top—always makes that decision."

"When we've been together for some time, I will. That takes trust, and it takes me knowing where your limits are."

She studied the selection again before selecting one from the middle. Not too thick, but one that would cover her eyes completely.

"Excellent choice. If it becomes too much, use your safe word."

Lizzie nodded. "I will."

Next, he picked up a small flogger.

Her heart stopped.

No matter how hard she tried, she couldn't look away from it…or his hand.

"Hold this for me, please?"

For a moment, she stared at it, wide-eyed, as if it were a serpent. She wasn't sure whether it was sent to tempt her or bite her.

With his head cocked to one side, he waited for her compliance.

This was a mind fuck. He had expectations of her, but she was able to say yes or no? After blowing out a breath that she hoped would clear the sudden fog in her brain, she accepted the handle.

It was thick and sturdy but lighter than she expected.

"Make a figure eight with your hand."

She did, and she watched the leather falls make a beautiful pattern.

"Now do it a little faster."

There was a difference in the sound and the feel. She glanced up at him.

"Yes. Exactly. It's capable of so many different sensations. And it can be mixed up also. Variety. Never knowing what to expect."

"I think I understand."

"You will. Oh, you will."

She lost her grip on the handle, but he caught the implement before it hit the hardwood floor.

After placing it on a shelf, he reached into the drawer for something else. "I have an additional suggestion for your first experience."

This was already too much to take in. How much wilder could he make it?

Braden pulled out a box.

Frantically she shook her head. "Candles?"

"Before you say no, have you ever played with wax?"

"When I was a kid, yes." *When I was younger and stupider.* "I'd pour it into my palm and roll it around."

"It cooled off quickly."

"Almost right away," she agreed. "But it stung like hell." Even though it caused no long-term damage.

"This is a different kind of wax. It burns at a much cooler temperature."

She pursed her lips. "I'm not convinced." But she didn't say no. Truthfully she'd enjoyed playing with wax, turning her hand so that the little melted puddle formed different shapes.

"Let's try this, then." He shook one of the candles out,

then picked up a lighter from the drawer and touched the flame to the wick.

Obstinately she placed her hands behind her back, and he smiled.

Then he extended his palm and drizzled a few drops on it before moving on to his forearm. He didn't flinch even once. "Try it?"

She was fascinated. Either he was working hard not to betray a reaction, or it really didn't hurt.

"Lizzie, you have a safe word. Or humor me."

"Fine." She extended one hand, and cleverly he clamped down on her wrist so she couldn't pull away.

In scared fascination, she watched him raise the tapered candle and slowly tip it to one side.

The first red drop seemed to fall forever. Then it landed, with the lightest, warmest of touches.

"Well?"

"My palm has thick skin." She'd liked it. But she had no idea where he planned to do it next. "It has to feel different on my naked body."

"Does it?"

Still holding her, he released another bit of wax, this time from a closer distance.

Even though it was warmer than the previous one, it was nothing like she'd experienced when playing with candles on her own.

Instantly the droplet hardened over.

"It looks beautiful. Doesn't it?"

The husky approval in his voice arced straight through her. And he was right. The way it combined with the other one was mesmerizing.

"Are you willing to try it on your forearm?"

"Yes," she whispered as she screwed her eyes closed.

Even though Braden chuckled, he was undeterred.

A tiny sting seeped into her, followed by another and another. She opened her eyes to see him stroking her with his thumb, making small concentric circles. "You were right."

He met her eyes. "How's that?"

"It's beautiful."

"What was the pain level, on a scale of one to ten?"

"Not much over a two." The way he was touching her, with possession wrapped around sensuality, was pretty close to a ten.

"Should we add it to tonight's play?"

"I want to try it."

"Anywhere I want?"

Breath vaporized from her lungs. *Anywhere?* It was about trust, but also about taking chances. A little part of her wanted to hold on to control. "I can still use my safe word if I change my mind?" She knew him well enough to guess where he was talking about.

"Of course. Always."

"If you mean it…" What was she getting into? "Yes."

His smile of approval made her giddy. It was very much part of his charm, and already she was becoming addicted to it.

"You're ready?"

On some level, she knew they'd already started, but she appreciated him being so purposeful. "I am." Her voice warbled so much that the words were almost unintelligible.

Lizzie drank in a little breath as he rewrapped her wrists.

Then, holding the ends of the tie, he drew her toward his bedroom. At the sight of his broad, strong back, her mind reeled. Being led like this—a true act of submission—was mind-blowing. Nerves collided with sensual awakening and shot a flood of heat through her.

When they reached the foot of the bed, he stopped. But

her body hummed with anticipation. He was her Top, and she was his very willing bottom.

"I want you to stand here without moving."

His words were phrased politely, but they had barbed wire beneath them, strong and pointed.

Lizzie remained where he indicated while he fetched the other toys from his closet and placed them on a nightstand. He left her alone in the room and then returned a minute later with a thick sheet of sorts.

Intrigued, she watched while he spread it on top of the comforter. She expected him to tell her to climb up onto it, but he didn't. Instead, he crossed to a chair and sat. "Come to me, Elizabeth."

The use of her full name startled her. He'd done it on purpose, she knew. He was changing their relationship, making it more formal, and it had a dizzying effect on her.

Her feet were leaden as she covered the short distance to stand before him, hands secured in front of her, exposed in a way she'd never been before.

"Good." He smiled again, and she took a breath she hadn't known she was holding.

His kindness gave her courage.

"Spread your legs wide."

He offered no assistance. Instead he sat there, expecting her obedience.

This whole thing was more emotionally challenging than she'd imagined it might be. But after hesitating for only a fraction of a second, she did as he said.

"I adore your trust." He trailed a finger up the inside of her right thigh and continued until he reached her pussy.

Lizzie moaned when he pulled away.

Then he rubbed between her labia. She wanted to hold on to him and bury her face in his shoulder. As if he knew that, he placed a restraining hand on her hip. With her hands tied, she was powerless to do much more than wiggle.

He stroked her and teased her, bringing her to the point of arousal again. Already he knew how to coax responses from her body.

"Now for your first spanking." He released the silken knot before assisting her over his lap. "Touch your fingers to the floor."

Once she was in position, he jostled her so that she was awkwardly perched, her rear end thrust into the air. Blood rushed to her face, and she knew it was more from embarrassment than from being upside down.

She tensed her muscles, anticipating his first spank and the sear of pain that would come with it.

As always, he surprised her. He caressed her thighs and buttocks, making her relax in ways that words would never accomplish.

Then he delivered dozens of small taps that turned her on.

"Do you like this?"

It was too humiliating to admit how much he was arousing her.

"Elizabeth?"

He paused as he waited for her answer. Cheeks heating, she nodded, but he still didn't continue. *"Yes."* It was a whisper, a confession.

He began rubbing her skin again, this time a little faster and harder than before. "You're doing well. Don't struggle against whatever is happening to you. Go with it."

Was he part mind reader?

He spanked her again, harder, then harder still. When she was whimpering, certain she couldn't take any more, he stroked her pussy, then slid a finger inside her.

"Oh!" She moaned. This was amazing. The spanking

pushed her somewhere deep inside her mind, but the way he toyed with her brought her back into her body. The combination was powerful. Suddenly she understood why so many people sought this out.

With slow strokes, he slipped his finger in and out of her, making her wet. She wriggled in a vain attempt to get him to go deeper inside her or bring her to orgasm.

"We'll go at my pace." He trapped her legs between his much more powerful ones, leaving her helpless.

She whimpered, and he rewarded her with another sharp dozen spanks and then going back deep inside her again with two fingers spread apart.

Overwhelmed, she cried out his name.

"Enough?"

"No!" Not even close.

From her peripheral vision, she saw him pick up the flogger. She tensed. But he did nothing more than trail the soft leather strands over her shoulders, down her back, across her thighs and ass cheeks before dangling them between her legs.

Then abruptly he tossed the toy onto the nightstand. Then, without speaking, he continued fucking her with his hand until she shattered, coming for him.

Her fingertips could no longer hold her up, and she collapsed, her palms on the floor for support. Tenderly Braden turned her over and gathered her against his chest.

Suddenly chilled, she snuggled into him.

"That was your first spanking."

Not wanting this heady feeling to go away, she remained where she was until her breathing returned to normal.

Before she was quite ready, he helped her up.

"I'd like you to sit at the foot of the bed, Elizabeth."

*That* tone… It was as uncompromising as it was forceful. Already, he had the ability to make her mind whirl into a place she'd never been before.

A little unsteadily, she managed the few steps that took her to the middle of the room. Braden remained where he was, watching her. Were her buttocks red? With as tender as her skin felt, they had to be.

Once she was perched on the edge, he stood and walked to her. "Scoot back a little."

With a little hip shimmy, something she was certain looked ungainly, she did.

"A bit farther, until your bottom is about eighteen inches from me."

Once he had her where he wanted her, he took hold of her shoulders and eased her down.

"Part your legs so I have access to your pussy."

Fighting off the instinctive embarrassment, she followed his order.

"Perfect. You'll be rewarded with extra spanks for that."

"What?" Extra spanks for behaving?

He left her to reach for the tie, and she turned her head to the side so she could follow his movements. While she watched in fascinated fear, he wrapped its length around one hand, then slowly unwound it before returning to drop it next to her waist.

Then he picked up the blindfold and offered it to her. "Put it on, Elizabeth."

This part was scarier than she'd imagined. Holding on to a vision of him, she placed the elastic band around her head, then secured the soft black material across her eyes.

"That's sexy. Now place your hands above your head."

Slowly she did, wondering where he was, what he was thinking. She was more aware of her body than she had ever been—her hard nipples, the waltz of goose bumps, the dampness between her legs, the scent of sex on her.

He tied her wrists together. "Go ahead and test the bonds."

She did, and there was very little slack. He slipped his finger between her skin and the fabric. Checking the fit for himself?

Light, stingy kisses assailed her, and she thrashed about.

He had to be using the flogger, and he was using it on every inch of exposed skin—her shins, ribs, shoulders, even her breasts. Not knowing where the tips would land was maddening. "I love it."

"And leather loves you, Elizabeth." He let the strands fall on her pussy—not hard, but enough to make her suck in her breath.

Then his mouth was on her, and he was licking her clitoris and pressing his tongue into her.

She needed to touch him and couldn't. She tossed her head from side to side, unsure if she was trying to escape or asking him to fill her completely.

His oral skills undid her, and she came against his mouth. "Braden!"

Relentlessly, he used the flogger *there* again, then soothed the hurt with another orgasm.

She lost track of the climaxes and hundreds, even thousands, of bites from his flogger. Lizzie was panting, begging, pleading, offering her whole body to him. She was his to take and use as he pleased.

Then suddenly his voice penetrated the now familiar place his sex games spiraled her into.

"Are you ready for what's next, Elizabeth?"

Lizzie froze. How could anything possibly exceed what they'd already done? No matter how apprehensive she was, she wanted to experience everything he had planned for her.

CHAPTER FIVE

*amn*. Before he pushed away from the bed, Braden took a moment to sweep his gaze over Lizzie's lush, naked body, pink from his flogger. Her long hair was sexy in its mussed disarray. In this moment of wild abandon, Lizzie was even more fucking spectacular than usual.

She tugged against her bondage as she sucked in shallow breaths, and she wiggled about, wordlessly seeking his touch.

His cock throbbed with incessant demand, but he forced himself to ignore it in favor of pleasing her.

He'd never interacted with anyone in quite this way. His reputation was well earned. Braden knew it, and while he wasn't proud of it, he'd done little to change it. When he scened, he did so with submissives at the local club, and when he dated, it was only with women who understood who he was and made relatively few demands on his time. He was happy to provide lavish gifts and expensive trips, but he'd been unfailingly frank about his decision to remain single.

Braden now realized it wasn't just his heart that he kept caged. He'd also extended the bars of his self-imposed jail around all of his emotions. Anger was a rare occurrence. He siphoned the energy from it and channeled it into making money. He spent time with Rafe Sterling and other Titans, members of the Zeta Society. But for the most part, he was content running his business and working out.

But Lizzie was different.

From the moment he saw her in his closet, something had been different for him. He wanted her with a fierceness he'd never experienced before.

After he kissed her, he realized it was more than that. The scent of her remained in his room and on his body.

At the party, she'd been every bit as in charge as the planner had been. She was competent and coolly collected. No doubt those were traits that made her great in her job as well. But they'd also be fabulous in a wife.

*Fuck.*

*A wife?*

Not once had he considered getting married. A few of his friends had fallen in love. Jaxon Mills had been the first to go, and damn, he'd toppled hard. He'd even heard rumors that Jack Quinn was smitten with Sinead O'Malley, an up-and-coming musician and songwriter from an enemy clan.

While Braden celebrated with his friends when they started looking at diamond rings, he silently questioned their sanity. Why bother? Half—or more—marriages ended in hellishly expensive divorces. And how many of the ones that lasted were happy unions? He had to look no further than his own parents for that answer. Married over thirty years. Living in separate houses for more than two decades. Not for him.

But Lizzie...

When he'd needed a break from his grandparents' celebration, he sought her out. Kissing her was spectacular. Her responses were honest and uninhibited. He couldn't wait to get her alone, and their connection grounded him. He liked having her in his house, and in his life, and especially his bed.

What would it take to keep her there?

Taking care not to tug on her hair, Braden removed her blindfold.

She blinked against the light and fixed her gaze on him before gifting him with a slow, soft smile.

"I want to watch your reactions." He stood to light the tapered candlestick. "Keep your legs spread. Unless you would like me to tie them for you?"

Frantically she shook her head, but she didn't protest or use a safe word. Which meant she trusted him.

While she watched, he drizzled some of the wax onto the front of his hand, offering her silent reassurance.

She pressed her lips together, and he waited for a pool of liquid to form before tipping the candle and spilling it all onto her belly.

With a moan, she arched her back. Braden swiped a finger through the wax to dissipate the heat and create an artistic swirl.

Rather than ask what she thought of it, he pressed his thumb to her clit.

"Oh..."

Lizzie was still every bit as damp as she had been earlier. It was unbelievably easy to turn her on, and that made him want to wring orgasm after orgasm from her.

He moved his hand higher, toward the hollow of her throat. With her mouth parted, she closed her eyes. "Keep them open."

"I'll try."

He moved his wrist to the left a bit to drizzle the melted wax onto her skin. As she panted, he continued, moving lower, between her breasts and rib cage, down her belly, to the top of her pubic bone.

She started to draw her thighs together.

"Elizabeth."

"Sorry," she whispered.

But he had no intention of touching her intimately…yet.

Braden continued down her right leg, then across to her left. She exhaled a shaky, relieved sigh. Without stopping, he went on, decorating his way back up the insides of her thighs.

This time, when he reached her pussy, he stopped to lick her. He fingered her, finding her G-spot, and then he continued to tongue her until she began thrusting her hips in feminine demand.

Braden pulled back then, parted her labia, and kissed her swollen clit with the wax.

"Oh sweet God!" Then she screamed Braden's name as she came.

He grinned. She was absolutely perfect for him. "We're not done."

"I'm not sure how much more I can take." Her eyes were wide, and she'd arched her back off the mattress.

"Let's find out, shall we?" Relentlessly he continued with the candle, moving his hand in various ways to cover swaths of her body, creating a work of art on her beautiful breasts. Then he toyed with her left nipple. "I remember you're sensitive."

"More than ever, after what we've already done."

He held the tip between his thumb and forefinger, then moved the candle closer than he had when he'd decorated her clit. Intentionally Braden drew out the moment, enjoying the sight of her as she stared, wide-eyed, waiting for him to act. "Do you want this, Elizabeth?"

"It's so…"

"Do you?"

She stared at the flame. "Yes."

Braden drizzled the wax on her imprisoned nipple.

This time, when she closed her eyes, he didn't insist she open them. He'd seen what he needed to through the worst of it. Excitement, even if it was laced with hesitation.

For minutes, he continued on, randomly marking her, never letting her know what to expect. Sometimes he was mere inches from her skin. At others, he was almost a foot away as he created a sensory experience he hoped she'd always remember.

While she was lost, murmuring soft sighs, he blew out the flame, then touched her knee. "I'll be right back."

She shook her head in silent protest.

As promised, he wasn't gone long. When he returned, he dabbed her pussy with a clean cloth, then wiped off the wax with a damp one. He spread her apart as he dried her. She appeared a little tender from their evening, and that made him grin. Tomorrow, there was no doubt she'd remember everything they'd shared.

"Are we going to have sex?"

"That's up to you."

"Thank God."

Deciding to leave the rest of his artwork in place, Braden dropped the cloth on the sheeting. "I'll take that in a positive way?"

"Yes!" Exasperation and urgency tinged her answer.

He took a condom from a drawer in the nightstand. "How are your arms?"

"They're fine." She shrugged a few times as if to prove it.

For a second he debated what to do. He'd enjoy having her sheath him. But keeping her tied appealed to his kinky side, and as a bonus, he'd be inside her faster. That thought swayed his decision.

He checked her bondage to be sure she hadn't lost circulation. Regardless, he didn't want to leave her much longer.

Which was fine. He wasn't sure how much longer he could wait to be inside her.

Lizzie stared at him as he removed his underwear.

"Oh."

"Oh?" He grinned.

*"Oh!"* She closed her legs. "That's... I mean you're..."

"I haven't had a lot of complaints." He rolled the condom down his cock, then captured her ankles and drew her toward him. "Lift your legs for me." He continued to guide her, until he had her in the position he wanted, with her ankles framing his head and her pelvis flush with his.

Braden inserted two fingers, moving them slowly in and out, spreading her, making sure she was ready for him before pressing his shaft against her entrance. "Breathe. We'll do this slowly."

She nodded. Once she took a breath, he slid his cockhead inside her, then immediately pulled back.

He repeated the motion again and again, going a little deeper with each stroke as she became wetter. Finally he thrust hard one last time and filled her completely.

In sweet invitation, her pussy muscles snuggled around him. They fit together well, and he'd happily do this with her every day for the rest of his life.

That realization almost made him lose control, so he stopped and feathered his fingers across her clit.

"Braden..." Her voice trailed off, and she pressed her mouth closed.

Slowly he once again began to move, and he leaned forward a couple of inches, forcing her legs apart and allowing him a little deeper inside her.

She whimpered.

"Too much?"

"I'm just... No. Close..."

He stroked her pussy harder and shortened his strokes,

ensuring he stayed deep, creating a cadence that would allow her to surrender. Then he reached for her left nipple and pinched it hard.

She arched her back, using her legs for leverage, and screamed as she orgasmed.

If there was a sweeter sound, he hadn't heard it.

As she rode out her climax, he murmured words of approval, letting her know how perfect she was.

Only then did he resume fucking her, losing himself in her sweetness.

Braden's balls drew up, and he gritted his back teeth as he ejaculated deep inside her.

He continued to hold on to her until his breathing returned to normal and he once again became aware of the world around him.

Lizzie was looking up at him. Her eyebrows were furrowed, and her head was tilted to one side as she studied him.

"I didn't know it could be like that," she admitted.

Neither did he. The connection he shared with her was unlike any other. For the first time in his life, a woman had gotten to him, made him consider a future.

Now that he'd found her, he didn't plan to let her go.

⁂

"I assure you, it's big enough for both of us."

Lizzie looked at Braden's enormous bathtub, and she knew he was right. The problem was, she didn't want to climb into the inviting water with him.

The sex they shared was magnificent, and her introduction to BDSM had exceeded all of her expectations. But what really ripped apart her carefully constructed world was the way he cared for her.

After he'd orgasmed, he untangled their bodies; then he released her wrists and rubbed her skin before helping her to lower each arm in turn.

Then he'd returned with a bottle of massage oil to remove the wax. While he cleaned up the bedroom, she rinsed off, then luxuriated in his steam shower. Then he filled the bathtub with water and invited her to join him.

He offered his hand.

Still, she paused. She was already wrapped in a towel and most of the way dry. It would be smarter to put some physical as well as emotional distance between them. But the truth was, she didn't want to. And what was her plan? To return to the guest room? Crawl back into his bed while he was in the bathroom?

All of a sudden, the turmoil of her emotions complicated things. The morning would arrive soon enough, and she could sort through her thoughts and feelings then. After everything they'd shared, what harm could come from spending another few minutes together?

Lizzie dropped the towel to accept his help, stepping into the far end of the tub, then bracing herself on the wall as she lowered herself into the depths.

"Come here. I want you in my arms."

She scooted into position, cradled between his strong thighs. Braden wrapped his arms around her and tucked her hair to one side as she rested the back of her head against his chest.

"Tell me about your experience."

*Do I have to?* She wrinkled her nose and was glad she was faced away from him so he couldn't see her.

As if he'd read her mind, he went on. "It's crucial to talk. Letting me know what you think, what worked, what didn't. It's all part of the experience."

"I never talked about sex before."

"Maybe not with others." His voice was soothing, helping push aside her inhibitions. "But you will with me."

His words were final, a decree more than a request. "It was..." *Life changing.* "Everything I hoped it could be."

"In specific, how was your spanking?"

Even though steam rose from the water, she shivered. "I'd be interested in trying it again." Even though it wouldn't, couldn't happen again.

"How about the flogger?"

"Weird."

He tightened his arms around her. "How so?"

"Like...it bites or stings, but it can also be gentle. I liked it."

"And the candle?"

"Exquisite. Hot, but not too much, and when it hardens, it becomes..." She frowned. "It's hard to explain. Tight on my skin." She'd never experienced such an onslaught of reactions. One drop was hardening as another formed.

"So everything we did would go on your list of approved activities?"

Lizzie nodded. Then her mind skipped ahead to a future that she'd already told herself was impossible. His reputation proved he was not a forever type of man, and she eventually wanted it all—marriage, a home, a baby or two.

But there was no rationalizing when it came to him. She wanted to know what other types of experiences were out there.

Braden brushed his knuckles up the column of her throat.

No other man had ever treated her like this. He'd set a standard that she wasn't sure anyone could live up to.

When he tightened his grip around her, the emeralds in his ring glinted. Asking about it would be safer than discussing sex or sifting through her messy, confused emotions. "I've been wondering about something."

"Hmm?"

"What's the significance of your owl?"

"This one?" He moved his finger.

She noticed he didn't give a direct answer. Was he stalling? "Yes. Rafe was wearing one that looked the same. And there's a picture of your dad in the study, shaking hands with the president. I can't be entirely certain, but they look like yours." When he still didn't answer, she pressed on. "Is it from a college fraternity or something?"

"Or something."

She twisted around so that she could look at him. His lips were set in a firm line, which meant he *was* stalling. Since that increased her curiosity, she pressed on. "It's different when I'm asking the questions, isn't it?"

"Lizzie, don't."

Even though he held up a hand as if to ward off her question, she refused to be deterred. "After everything we've shared, the trust I showed you, I think I deserve an answer."

After a few more seconds, he sighed. "I belong to an organization known as the Zetas."

Lizzie frowned. "I've never heard of it."

"Not many people have. That's intentional."

Realization dawned. "You're not talking about a secret society or something, are you?" That couldn't be possible. Though she'd read about such things, she didn't really believe them.

When he didn't answer, she scooted back a little farther, sending water cascading over the edge of the tub. Ignoring the mess, she studied his cool gray eyes intently. "Are you serious right now?"

He shrugged. "I'm not at liberty to say."

"Hypothetically, then…" Lizzie wasn't sure how to phrase her question. "If secret societies actually existed, would the Zetas be among them?"

"That's quite a reach."

But he hadn't said no.

Suddenly it became clearer to her. Her mother's evasiveness. His study. The dozens of photographs featuring Braden's grandfather and father with other notable people. The owl on the desk. The Z symbol on the rings and on a banner. "You *are* a member of a secret society. What do you do, rule the world?"

"Something like that."

"Are you going to tell me more?" She scooted even farther away, intentionally putting distance between them when he reached for her.

"Jesus, Lizzie. Can you let it go?"

"We slept together," she reminded him again.

"Are you always this tenacious?"

"Don't play word games with me." She shook her head in warning and continued to stare at him.

When he remained silent, chill bumps formed on her arms. She pushed to her knees, fully intending to climb out of the tub.

Braden snagged her wrist and held her gently. "The Zeta Society is a membership group, yes. And we don't publicly talk about it. So that makes it secret, I suppose. But that doesn't mean it's something nefarious."

"So what it is?"

"Mostly, it's a group of people who do good in the world. Or try to."

"Mostly?"

He smiled, but it didn't ease the tension in her. "You would seize that word."

"So what else is it?"

He rubbed his thumb across her pulse point. Despite her inner turmoil, she began to relax.

"The organization was formed in the 1800s by a group of

men who were in a secret college fraternity. Years later, they decided to help each other in various ways—referrals, business loans, that sort of thing."

"Why do I feel as if you're leaving out part of the story?"

"We have a long list of charitable causes. Every year, we have a two-week event on our estate in Louisiana. Members from all over the globe come for various lengths of time. We discuss geopolitical events and exchange ideas. Hopefully we make the world a little better. It's all very informal. A few workshops. And because we're in the same place at the same time, we get to spend time with people we wouldn't ordinarily see. And like any organization, there's a small group who run it. In this case, it's a steering committee." He shrugged. "And it's my understanding it's every bit as boring as it sounds. Inviting speakers to the annual meeting, approving membership requests, coordinating volunteers for charity events."

"You're not telling me the interesting parts."

"That's all there is to it." He allowed the words to hang in the air for a moment. "Except for the bonfire and the sacrifice."

Her eyes widened.

"That's a joke. Well, the sacrifice is, anyway."

She couldn't tell fact from fiction. "I'll find out on the internet."

"There won't be much there. If you have specific questions, come to me."

"You're not exactly forthcoming."

"I'll tell you more as time goes on."

This wasn't the first time he'd mentioned them continuing a relationship, which was something she couldn't allow to happen.

Braden released her; then he flipped the lever to drain the tub. "Say you'll come back to bed with me, Lizzie."

Once again, he was using her less formal name. The way he switched between Elizabeth and Lizzie affected her in different ways, and each made her vulnerable to him.

"Please?"

She was helpless to resist his power over her.

He climbed out of the bath and shucked the water from his skin before grabbing a fresh, fluffy towel for her.

After drying her off, he led her to the bedroom.

While she was in the shower, he'd removed the temporary sheeting and turned back the comforter. He'd also turned off the lights except for a dim lamp on the nightstand. There was a condom next to it. All along, he'd planned to seduce her again.

And it worked.

He lifted her up onto the mattress, then followed her.

This time, after giving her a couple of orgasms, he donned the condom, then rolled onto his back and drew her on top of him.

"Ride me, Lizzie."

This was something else she'd never done. And she didn't need to tell him that. Without saying anything, he held her around the waist, keeping her steady while she lowered herself on him.

Her pussy was sore from his flogger, his licking, kissing, melted drops of wax, and their hot sex. Braden's cock was exceptionally thick and long. Earlier she'd been unable to find the words to tell him that he was much larger than anyone else she'd been with. She was grateful they'd taken a bath together; otherwise she wasn't sure she'd be able to do this right now.

Once she found the right position, straddling him and leaning slightly forward, she began to ride him, taking a bit at a time, then raising herself back up.

Being in control was powerful, and she liked it.

"Exactly right." He cupped her breasts and squeezed them, driving her wild.

The slightest bit of pain increased her pleasure ten times. She tossed her head, losing herself in the unique sensations.

He gripped her a little tighter, and an orgasm rushed through her. Seconds later, she was pinned beneath him, and he was fucking her hard as he looked down at her.

"Put your hands over your head for me."

He wouldn't be denied, nor did she want to test him. Obeying him completely, she lifted her arms, and he pinned her wrists to the mattress.

In a primitive way that needed no words, he possessed her. He captured her mouth in a searing kiss, and they came at the exact same moment.

A wild energy rocked through her. She'd met all of his Dominant demands with every part of herself, holding nothing back.

Then, after a final shudder claimed him, he rolled to the side and tucked her against him. "You're mine, sweet Lizzie. Make no mistake."

His words rocked her. She was certain he meant what he said at that moment, while blinded by the heat of passion.

No doubt he said them to every woman he bedded. But that didn't stop her from tucking them away so she could replay them again later.

When Braden snuggled her close, she gave herself over to him, determined to enjoy their remaining moments together. In a few hours, she would go back to her real life and force herself to forget him.

CHAPTER SIX

"How about dinner tonight, Lizzie?"

Oh God. *Yes. No.* She'd been hoping and fearing that he would ask. This was the moment she'd been dreading. Since she couldn't find the strength to respond, she remained silent.

This morning, she'd awakened in his bed, trapped in the comfort of his arms. And she hadn't wanted to move.

She expected to feel some embarrassment from the night before, but she hadn't. Instead, she was at peace in a way she hadn't been for years. Having sex, scening with him, had been inevitable, at least for her. From the moment she'd been in his closet and discovered he was a Dominant, she'd wanted to experience everything he had to offer.

Knowing she had to protect herself, she'd slipped from his arms and escaped to the closet. By the time he threw back the sheet and sat up, she was dressed and ready to leave.

Braden dragged his hand through his hair in apparent confusion before suggesting they go out to breakfast. Politely she refused, saying she had a lot to get done since she'd spent all of Saturday helping her mother prepare for the party.

Even though she would have preferred to go home before coffee, he popped a couple of frozen waffles in the toaster oven. Those she wanted. Her mother had made them, and they were Lizzie's favorite. She was tempted to text her mom and ask for a stash of her own. But that would mean admitting she was at Braden's house.

After eating, she picked up her phone to arrange for a ride, but Braden had been adamant that he was taking her home. His arms were folded, and it wasn't worth the argument.

The drive to her downtown house took under fifteen minutes, and the conversation in his luxury SUV was awkward. At the curb, she thanked him for the ride, then all but leaped out of the vehicle and hurried up the sidewalk.

She shouldn't have been surprised when he followed.

"Lizzie?"

With a trembling hand, she stuck the key in the lock, but she refused to turn it. If she opened the door, she might weaken and invite him in. Instead, standing there on the stoop, she turned back to face him.

"There's a seafood restaurant that Rafe recommends. I'm sure I can get reservations. How's seven?"

"I'm sorry, Braden." She shook her head even as she told herself there was nothing to apologize for. He was merely going through the polite formalities that happened after he slept with a woman.

Or maybe he meant it when he said he wanted to see her again. Perhaps he'd enjoyed the sex as much as she did and actually did want to hook up again.

But she had her rules about relationships. Career first. Men second, and then only if they were interested in something long-term. And his reputation proved he was not. Seeing the world's most scandalous billionaire again would no doubt lead to certain—and maybe unrecoverable—heartbreak.

"Lizzie—"

"Don't." She offered a weak smile that faded as quickly as it formed. "Please. I enjoyed it, Braden. Really. But…"

"But?"

Wishing he would leave didn't magically make him disappear. "Can't we leave it at this? We had a nice evening—"

"Nice?"

She swallowed. "It was great. Okay?" Lizzie was stumbling all over her words. "Going out, like on a date, is a bad idea."

Like he had earlier in the day, he folded his arms, making him bigger, more intimidating, and damn it, more appealing too. Today he wore jeans and a tight T-shirt that showed off his strong arms, making her remember the way he'd captured her and spanked her.

"You want to fuck instead?"

Oh God. *"No!* That's not what I said." Intentionally he was twisting her words.

"You came for me, multiple times. You slept in my arms the entire night. What happened between last night and this morning?"

Lizzie glanced around to be sure none of the neighbors were watching. She didn't want to have a scene here, but she still refused to invite him in. Braden, on the other hand, seemed not to give a damn about anything other than getting the answers he wanted. "Look, not everything needs to be discussed. Let's agree to be friends. We can pretend it never happened."

"Absolutely no fucking way, Lizzie. It happened. I'm taking responsibility for it, and so are you."

"Agreed." She gave him a second smile, this one so wide

and fake that it hurt her face. "Responsibility taken." Her voice cracked. "Thank you for a great experience."

"I'd like an explanation. What did I do wrong?"

*Nothing.* In fact, he'd done everything right. His behavior was perfect, so smooth that he'd obviously spent years practicing it.

"Talk to me, Lizzie." Then he refolded his arms, the gesture a little uncertain, as if he wasn't certain exactly what to do.

More than anything, that got to her. Maybe if she was honest with him, he'd show her some mercy and not contact her again. "I'm not going to be one of your numerous women, Braden."

"What the..." His nostrils flared and his biceps bulged, as if he was fighting back anger. "Is that what you think?"

Shocked by his reaction, she blinked.

When he spoke again, his voice was sharp with accusation. "You're fucking making that up."

"No. I'm not. And I resent your implication that I'm lying." Anger raced through her, but she wouldn't slow down to take a breath. Instead, she rushed on. "I've seen what happens to the women you're involved with. You...you fuck them in the back of limousines and then smile for the cameras when you're caught. I won't have my name dragged through the muck in the gossip rags. I have to work for a living. I have a job that matters to me, one that I can't lose. My reputation matters."

He took a step toward her, but she stood her ground.

Convincing herself that she needed to end this was as difficult as convincing him. "More than anyone you should understand that I'm not from your world. Secret societies, scandalous liaisons that don't have real-world consequences."

Finally she drew that much-needed gulp of air. "You probably know that my dad abandoned us. My mom spent most of her time at your house, and I saw how many hours she worked to take care of me. She made endless sacrifices. We lived with family members, and the two of us shared a bedroom." Lizzie forced herself to go on. "I swore I wouldn't make bad choices when it came to men. I don't date a lot, and I never have casual sex. I'm not willing to settle for anything less than total commitment from any man." Tears built in her eyes, but she refused to spill them. "Last night meant something to me. And that's why it can't happen again. I can't be number six thousand on your list of one-night stands." *Fuck, fuck. Don't cry. Do not cry.*

"You know, Lizzie"—his voice was low, dangerously so—"I'm damn tired of you insulting me. The other day, you intimated that I would fire your mother because you were in my closet." He leaned toward her, so close that she could feel the heat that came off him in waves. "You don't know a goddamn thing about me. Yeah. You're right that I've made mistakes. A pile of them that I regret. But sleeping with you is not among them. And you're wrong—so very wrong—if you think it meant nothing to me."

She wanted to believe him, but she couldn't take a risk that he wasn't being truthful. After all, he had a reputation. He knew women. He knew *her*.

"You're special, Lizzie. What we shared was spectacular, and so was the trust you placed in me. I want to take you out —see where this goes, give you a chance to see for yourself who I really am instead of believing salacious narrative crafted by the paparazzi. Fuck it all. I deserve it. We deserve it."

"I'm..." *Tempted.* So very tempted. But she couldn't take a chance on being ensnared in his web with no way out.

While she was still able, Lizzie turned away. While she fumbled with the lock, he made no move to help her.

Finally, the tumblers fell into place.

"Lizzie, please."

"Goodbye, Braden." She dashed inside and slammed the door closed. With a flick of her wrist, she slid the deadbolt into place before collapsing against the wall and letting her tears fall in a rush of anguish.

⌘

Braden had never allowed himself to get stupid over a woman. He didn't drown his sorrows, never mourned the loss of a relationship.

But this time was different.

This time the woman in question was Lizzie.

And he was no longer on top of his game.

Rafe had arrived at the downtown bar near Buffalo Bayou several minutes ahead of Braden. He'd already chained up his bike and removed his helmet when Braden rode up.

"Pull a muscle or something?" Rafe asked.

Braden ignored the question. He'd poked at Rafe in the past when he was first smitten with Hope. Now that things were different, Braden wasn't as jovial.

After securing his own bike and unfastening the strap beneath his chin, he followed Rafe inside the bar. The host waved them in when they said they wanted their usual table on the patio.

Fans hung from the overhead beams, and the blades churned through the humid late-afternoon air.

"Business problems?" Rafe asked when they both had cold glasses of beer in front of them.

"No." That was fine. "Better than usual." Maybe because of the hours he'd been putting in. Generally he took a few evenings off a week, but since Lizzie had closed the door in his face almost a month ago, he'd worked eighteen hours a day, and twenty on several occasions.

Rafe took a drink and waited.

Irritated, Braden slammed his glass onto a coaster. "What's to say there's something wrong?"

"Besides your riding speed and the fact your eyeballs look like you dragged them across sandpaper?" Rafe took a drink. "Or perhaps it's your general asshole-ish attitude. If we wanted that, we could have invited Jax."

Jaxon Mills was an internet marketing guru, and Braden didn't understand the man's appeal. *Asshole* was a great word for him. His staunchest allies said he was blunt, even to the point of rudeness—but that he was only being honest and telling people what they needed to hear. Some called him a motherfucker. Still, people who did as he ordered tended to have extraordinary success. He had some sort of intuition that the rest of the planet lacked. And recently, he'd taken a mighty fall from the sacred bachelorhood platform. Of course, he'd done it in Jaxon style, telling the entire world Willow was the world's greatest woman. He ranted about how fortunate he was and how his recent marriage was the best in the history of the planet.

"Gonna tell me about it? Or should we just stare at one another as we get drunk?"

This was tricky. Lizzie was more than just the woman he was obsessed with—she was one of Rafe's most important employees.

"It's under lock and key."

The reference to the bond shared by the members of the Zeta Society reassured him. "It's Lizzie."

"Ah." Rafe took a long drink.

"What the fuck does that mean?"

"She asked to be transferred after the Uptown Sterling opens. Makes more sense now."

"She…" Braden put down the glass he'd just picked up.

"You didn't know?"

How the hell would he? She hadn't taken his calls, and her mother didn't talk about her, even when he asked. "She's not interested in me."

"That's not the impression I had when I saw you two together at your grandparents' party."

That was true. The chemistry they shared was combustible. "Seems my reputation is a problem for her."

"What are you going to do about it?"

"The fuck does that mean?" Braden scowled.

"If a man has changed, how would the woman he wants know that? How could she trust it?"

"Roses?"

"Works with some." Rafe shrugged. "I tried it myself. Painful experience. You ever been in a flower shop? Once is enough." He took another fortifying drink. "But would the woman in question think he's just trying to get back in her good graces?"

Was that what he'd be trying to do?

She'd accused him of being a philanderer. And maybe that was true. Or it had been, until her. From the moment they reconnected, something had changed in him. Lizzie wasn't like any other woman. She was honest, and she'd hidden none of her reactions from him. But there was more. Lizzie was authentic. Over the years, they'd spent hours talking at the kitchen counter. In all that time, she'd never changed. Instead, she'd blossomed into more of who she was. He admired her determination to hold on to that.

"Can you blame her?"

"What?" Braden shook his head to bring himself back to the conversation.

"Some women don't want flowers or pretty words. They need commitment."

Lizzie had been absolutely clear about that.

Rafe signaled for the server to bring them another round. "There's a tradeoff. Always."

"My parents. Yours. Fuck, even Jaxon's." Rafe's dad had taken off with a younger woman, almost wrecking the family business. Jaxon had grown up in such a screwed-up, dysfunctional house that it was amazing he was even halfway normal.

"No one would blame you if you keep doing what you're doing."

Their fresh drinks arrived. As Braden picked up his glass, he studied Rafe. "You happy?"

"Yeah." Rafe took a long drag from his glass. "Never thought I wanted to be married, but…" He met Braden's eyes as he shrugged. "Here I am. I like having a partner, someone to talk to. It's nice waking up next to her."

Nice wasn't a word Braden used a lot. But damn it, having Lizzie in his arms every morning would be spectacular.

"And there's her damn cat." Rafe grinned stupidly.

"A cat?" *Seriously?* "A cat?"

"The Colonel. Though she may be due for a promotion soon. She's even more bossy than ever."

"An actual real life *cat?*" What in the actual hell had happened to his friend. "Earth to Rafe."

"I'll give it to you straight." Rafe managed to stop grinning. "Being with a woman who has your back?" He shook his head. "Makes everything worthwhile. My friend, you need to choose your path. Do you want to walk it alone?"

The conversation turned to business, the Astros baseball team, then to football. After nachos and street tacos, they said their goodbyes. Rafe was going straight home while Braden wanted to work off some of his tension.

Hours later, he was forced to admit the exercise hadn't helped.

"Do you want to go with me to my aunt's this evening?" Lizzie asked Crystal after they collapsed on the patio of a local restaurant, following their latest outing. Because Lizzie had been so distraught since she left Braden's home, she'd kept herself occupied with yoga and working out with her trainer. And she'd gone shopping more times than she cared to count.

"Oh my God. Tell me it's not Triple T night."

"Yeah. It is." For Lizzie, it was likely to be heavy on the tequila.

"I knew I shouldn't have procrastinated on my chores. I love your aunt's tacos."

"You might be able to talk Aunt Virginia into giving you a to-go box, and then you wouldn't have to worry about tomorrow's lunch. That would save you some time."

"Damn, girl. You know how to tempt me."

"But no, right?" The truth was, Lizzie would appreciate her friend providing a distraction. Her mother had noticed Lizzie's listlessness and the tears in her eyes each time she held Sandra's newborn. Lizzie always managed to make her getaway before Mom could corner her, but earlier Eileen texted to say she wanted to talk. Lizzie's time was up. And she had no idea what she was going to say.

"Is your man still calling you?"

"Braden Gallaher is not my man!"

Crystal leaned forward. "But you want him to be."

"That's not true."

"Oh, girl. You're lyin' and you know it." Crystal grinned.

"Fine." Her friend was right, even if Lizzie didn't want to admit it. "Yes. I've heard from him." Twice, he'd sent flowers to her office. She'd promptly put them on the front desk for others to enjoy and so that she didn't have to think about him every time she looked at them or inhaled their fragrance.

"So what's the problem? Is he ugly?"

"No." She shook her head with a grin. "Definitely not. A full-on hottie."

Crystal picked up a napkin and waved it in front of her face. After they both succumbed to a round of giggles, she tried again. "Okay… He has to be craptacular in bed, right?"

"No!"

"Ha! So you did sleep with him!"

Instead of answering, Lizzie looked away to hide her embarrassment.

"Still not seeing what the problem is. Oh, wait! He's unemployed. Bastard needs to get a job."

"He's loaded." In the days right after he took her home, she'd spent hours doing research about him. She learned Braden hadn't followed his dad into the family business, but rather, he went to work for a brokerage firm, then started his own company when he attained a seven-figure income.

Even though she had no doubt his influential friends allowed him access to their portfolios, the service he offered was unique. He spent his days talking to people, flying around the world, connecting investors with opportunities, some which were incredibly risky but carried great potential.

Unable to stop herself, she'd also looked into the Zeta Society. There was precious little on the internet about the society except for a couple of articles, including one from the 1930s. An enterprising reporter had seen several high-profile men in New Orleans for some sort of gathering, and he'd called them Titans. According to more recent reports, the nickname had stuck. Members were from all over the world, and they evidently had some sort of meeting every year, with a bonfire as one of the highlights. Though it was rumored that some of the world's most elite leaders and entrepreneurs belonged to the organization, there was no confirmation.

"I'm running out of things here."

Crystal's voice broke into Lizzie thoughts, and she shook her head.

"Help me out. The guy is handsome, good in bed, and he's loaded." Crystal scowled. "So why are you avoiding him? Was he mean to you? Is that it? He better not have been, 'cause I'll deck him."

The image of five-foot-nothing Crystal taking on the tall, fit Braden was comical.

"Talk to me, Lizzie."

"I don't want to be girlfriend number six thousand."

"Oh." Crystal stabbed her straw in her diet soda. "Well, fuckydoodle."

*"Girlfriend* is a loose term. It's more like he has a series of affairs."

"And you're only about forever, right? Happily ever after, babies and all that. You were right to dump him."

Was that what she had done? It didn't feel like that to her. "Well, anyway, I told Rafe that I'm up for a transfer once my assignment at the Sterling Uptown is over." It might be another two or three months, which definitely seemed a lifetime away.

"Where are you considering?"

When she traveled for extensive periods, Crystal often joined Lizzie. She arranged comped rooms, and as a result, they'd spent time in a number of different cities, including a couple abroad. "Not sure yet."

"Ask for Singapore."

An overseas appointment intrigued her. Right now, she'd like to put as much distance between her and Houston as possible.

"Make sure it's exotic." Crystal stabbed her drink again. "White sandy beaches, frozen cocktails."

They chatted for a few minutes before Lizzie announced she needed to leave so she'd be on time for dinner at her aunt's house.

Once she was inside, noise and mayhem surrounded her. Someone was yelling, "Shots, shots, shots!" in the dining room. The tweens and teenagers were blasting a video game in the living room, and somewhere in the distance, Sandra's baby wailed. Sunday evening at Aunt Virginia's. Lizzie grinned.

She greeted friends and family members as she headed for one of those jiggers of tequila. Being here was exactly what she needed to throw off the shroud of melancholy that had dropped on her shoulders while she was talking to Crystal.

With the alcohol warming her insides, Lizzie headed to the kitchen, looking for her mother. Might as well get the unwanted conversation over with before the tequila buzz faded and she had to drive home.

Lizzie picked up a towel and began drying the dishes her mom had just rinsed.

"Something's bothering you. Work issues? I met your boss that day, you know. At the Gallaghers' party. He said very nice things about you. So it can't be that."

"It's not."

"Man problems?" Eileen guessed.

Lizzie wasn't squeamish about discussing relationship troubles with her mother, but the fact that she was employed by Braden made it more delicate.

When Lizzie didn't respond right away, Eileen grinned. "I knew it."

"What?" So she didn't drop the glass she was holding, Lizzie set it in the dish drainer.

"He's a good man."

"Who?" She turned her back to the counter so she could look at her mom better.

"Oh, honey. It's clear to everyone. Braden."

Lizzie had never been able to hide anything from her mother. She wasn't sure why she even tried.

"He needs a good woman."

"I don't know about that. He's got a million or so hanging around."

"Are you certain?"

Her mother would know. "But... I found his tie in the living room. Underneath the couch."

"Did you ask him about it?"

"Are you telling me there's a simple explanation and that the woman might not be one of his..." She struggled for the right word. "Conquests?"

"I think it's easy to make judgements. How well do you really know him?"

She didn't. Not really. "He did tell me he's a member of the Zeta Society."

"Oh? Hmm."

"Hmm, what?"

"To my knowledge, he's never shared that with anyone else. As for conquests, why don't you talk to Braden? If he's told you that much, he's not keeping secrets.

"What do you know?" Lizzie dropped the dish towel she'd been holding.

Eileen pressed her lips together. That she'd said that much was surprising and made Lizzie's mind spin a hundred different directions.

"I know it was difficult for you not having a father, and I'm sorry about that. But don't let my mistakes poison your future." Eileen touched Lizzie's wrist. "Look around here. There are plenty of honorable men. You deserve happiness."

Just then, Sandra entered the kitchen, carrying her beautiful baby. And Lizzie extended her arms to accept the sleeping child.

Throughout the rest of the evening, her mother's words flitted through Lizzie's thoughts. Each time, she shoved them away. Braden was not the man for her.

She arrived home to a chilled and dark house, a sharp contrast to her aunt's bright and welcoming home.

When she finally fell asleep after hours of tossing and turning, her dreams were tortured by thoughts of Braden, and the horrifying realization that she'd let fear and doubt stand in her way rather than giving him a chance.

CHAPTER SEVEN

Halfway up the driveway, Lizzie stopped her car in shock.

Braden was on her front doorstep, pacing back and forth, his dark hair raked back and his blue tie askew. She wasn't sure he'd ever looked more handsome.

For long moments, she sat there, debating what to do.

But he made the decision easier. Obviously sensing her indecision, he jogged down the steps and followed the path leading to the driveway. Then he shoved his hands into his pockets and waited while she moved the gear shifter into Park.

He rocked back and forth as he waited for her to exit, and when she did, he took a respectful step back.

"Lizzie…" His voice cracked, and so did the ice around her heart.

How long had he been here, standing outside in the relentless Houston heat and humidity?

"I—" He gave a rueful grin. "Fuck it all."

She waited, eyebrows drawn together.

"I knew what I wanted to say to you. And I had a speech all prepared. Well, Jaxon helped me with it."

"Jaxon?"

"Jaxon Mills. You know, the internet star who has magical woo-woo words for every occasion."

"I adore him." And Braden for taking a risk and asking his friend.

"But now that I'm here... And I look at you, how beautiful you are. How much you mean to me." He exhaled and rocked forward onto the balls of his feet. "I can't remember a damn single word that I wanted to say, and I'm screwing this all up." He swallowed. "If you tell me to leave, I promise I'll never contact you again."

That was definitely the safer option. But since she'd seen him last, she'd been an emotional wreck. It was difficult to believe that an actual breakup could be any worse. The time she spent with him had been wonderful, and she knew that if they were together, there would be dozens, hundreds of other experiences that would be equally spectacular.

If she refused to take a risk, she might not have further pain, but she'd also miss out on the joy.

In the end, which was worse?

"I've missed you, Lizzie." The words were spaced out, and they were jagged with emotion. "At night, I walk around the house, lost. When you were there, I had a sense of comfort. But now..."

"Now?"

"It's not a home without you."

*Home.* Those things she wanted.

"A couple of weeks ago, I met up with Rafe. We had a long talk."

"About what?"

"My reputation, mostly."

"The Scandalous Billionaire."

He winced. "You were right to walk away, even though it devastated me."

*It had?*

When he continued, raw honesty roughened his words. "I've never had a long-term relationship, never wanted one. Until now."

Her stomach tumbled.

"You know my parents had a fucked-up marriage—hell, it still is. For more than twenty years, they've lived in separate houses without communicating. They're both stuck in their grief, blaming each other for my sister's death."

And neglecting Braden.

"But the truth is, there are good examples of committed relationships. I just haven't been looking for them."

Did she dare hope?

"I really am screwing this up." For a few seconds he was silent. "I'm hoping you'll be willing to take a chance on me, make my reputation a thing of the past."

"What does that mean?" As a form of protection, she wrapped her arms around herself.

"That I want forever with you."

"You…"

Right then, in her driveway, mindless of anyone who might drive by or be outside watching, he dropped to one knee. "I love you, Lizzie."

Stunned, she reached for the car door to steady herself.

A part of her had adored him for years, since the time he was kind to her when she was younger, less confident.

Braden reached into his suit jacket. "Will you marry me?" He pulled out a ring with a gigantic diamond.

The sun reflected off the gem, refracting a thousand different directions. Mesmerized by shock, she stared at the twinkling facets.

"Lizzie? For God's sake, say something."

She shook herself and met his gaze. "Why?"

He blinked. "Why?"

"I... I didn't expect this." She shook her head. Not in a million years. "Braden, you don't need to do this. We can date." She blushed. "Have sex."

"You're the one, Lizzie. I don't want to date you or have an affair with you. You're the woman I want to marry, to cherish and adore for all eternity."

"You want...?" The picture he created was one she wanted, with all of her being. Yet she still tried to be practical. One of them needed to be. "We don't know each other that well."

"Is that true? I've known you most of my life. I know you're honest. You have integrity. And damnably high standards." He smiled up at her. "You'll demand that your husband behave in a certain way. And I want to be that man for you. I want to be the father of your children. Let me prove myself worthy of you every single day."

"Braden..." Her heart threatened to explode with love she was trying to contain.

"Marry me, Elizabeth—Lizzie—Ryan."

"But... But..." Unable to think, she stood there, blinking.

"Do you love me?"

"It's not that easy."

"Tell me what you're thinking."

"There are complications. I love my job, and I put in for a transfer." But how could she leave Braden now that she'd found him?

"We can figure it out. I can work from almost anywhere, or you can fly home from time to time. I'm not asking you to give up anything, I'm asking you to let me give you more than you ever imagined. There's a reason I never committed before. I could never walk away from my wife. Marriage is a forever thing."

Which was what she wanted. After what he'd gone through, she believed him. He would never abandon her or their children. Lizzie closed her eyes, wanting to pinch herself. Was it truly possible for dreams to come true?

"Be my bride? The other half of me? The one I go through life with?"

"Yes. Yes." A thousand times. A thousand times a thousand. "I love you, Braden Gallagher."

He slipped the ring on her finger, and the fit was perfect. Honestly, she didn't care about the diamond. She cared about the man.

Then he stood. "I have champagne chilling in a cooler in my car."

Of course he did.

He took a couple of steps toward his vehicle, then stopped and came back. Seeing him uncertain made her heart swell even more.

"I didn't think this through." He shrugged. "I want to carry you into the house…but we have the champagne."

"Can it wait?"

He quirked an eyebrow in a way that let her know he was interested in what she had to say.

"I'd rather have you."

"The champagne can wait…but I can't!"

He closed her car door before scooping her from the ground.

"You can't do this!" She kicked and squirmed, but he tightened his grip, holding her close against his chest. "Braden!"

"Be still, woman!"

His fierce growl sent shockwaves through her. "Or what, Mr. Gallagher, Sir?"

"You're about to find out."

There was both threat and promise in his words.

He carried her up the path, toward the house and the future that suddenly looked much brighter than she could have imagined.

EPILOGUE

A calendar reminder vibrated Lizzie's watch. Since she was already in the Sterling Uptown hotel's posh but empty lobby, she dismissed the notification and continued walking toward the specialty coffee and confectionary shop.

Though she reached La Patisserie five minutes early, Rafe was already there, occupying a small table at the far corner, next to a large window. He had a porcelain cup in front of him, along with a plate adorned with several macarons, each a different color—yellow, orange, and light purple. His head was bent, and he was jotting something on his phone screen.

Because Lizzie had been up since well before dawn and had consumed enough coffee to power her through a week or more, she went to the counter and ordered a sparkling mineral water with a slice of fresh lime.

Still ahead of schedule, she pushed down her nerves and headed for her boss, who looked up before tucking his high-tech device inside his jacket pocket. She'd worked for him for years, so she shouldn't be nervous about their meeting. But he'd only sent her a request a couple of hours ago, and as far as she knew, his visit to the property hadn't been planned.

Generally when he dropped by, they met in her office. The irregularity of the situation made her wonder if something was wrong.

"Ah, Elizabeth. There you are." Rafe pushed back his chair and half stood while she took her seat. "Thanks for making the time."

As if she had a choice. "Of course."

"I know this is inconvenient."

Instead of replying, she squeezed the juice from the piece of fruit into her glass. She had a million details to oversee for the property's numerous upcoming festivities. Their first event was this evening—a gathering of VIPs, most of them Titans—hosted by Braden.

They'd worked together on the details, and in addition to overseeing the function, she was cohosting with him, her first as his future wife.

The fact she intended to marry a member of the Zeta Society still boggled her mind.

Rafe glanced around the bright, airy café. "Every detail is perfect."

It was. There were half-round booths, the backs covered with bright pink material. The scattered tables had fanciful feet and legs, and striped-fabric chairs were pushed beneath them. Apothecary jars of various shapes and sizes adorned the glass shelving attached high on one wall.

"The team you hired did a great job."

While she appreciated his approval, she'd merely executed his idea. He'd spared no expense to make this property one of the finest in the chain.

Houston was a rapidly growing cosmopolitan city. Dignitaries, businesspeople, actors, and rock stars demanded the Uptown's type of extravagance and pampering. On all fronts, he had delivered.

After staring at the cookies for a while, he asked if she'd like one.

"Thanks, but no. I did a sampling the other day." She'd need to hit the elliptical machine if she ate another one.

"Which do you suggest I start with?"

"If you like floral, I recommend the purple one. It's lavender and rose." With a to-die-for buttercream filling.

After studying the choices, Rafe picked up the one she suggested and took a hesitant bite. "Wow." Then he dropped the cookie. "Uhm... Yeah. It tastes like flowers."

"I wasn't kidding, and I agree, it's a bit unexpected." Lizzie smiled. "The orange with chocolate-bourbon ganache may be more to your liking." The pastry chef, trained in Paris, was renowned for her unusual combinations. Additionally she planned to add seasonal flavors, including pumpkin spice for fall, candy-cane mocha for winter, mint julep for the Kentucky Derby, strawberry shortcake and limeade for summer. Repeat customers would always find something new to savor.

"I'll pass." Rafe nudged the plate toward her. "How much do we charge for those?"

"Ten dollars for three." As she eyed the delicacies, her resistance began to crumble. "It's a discount over buying them individually."

"We can get that for something so small?"

"All day long." Starting at five a.m. On the weekends, the café would be open until midnight for late-night snacking. In addition to cookies, Chef had plenty of other choices including crème brûlée, tarts, petits fours, miniature cakes. "We anticipate guests will add a specialty coffee or tea, or even a glass of wine, bringing the average check to twenty dollars." Which was a savings over ordering a couple of desserts at their restaurants.

He nodded. "And worth every penny?"

"Not everyone can make exceptional pastries. And these? They're a bargain."

"I trust you when it comes to pricing of"—he looked at the purple thing—"macaroons."

"These are macarons." Despite the consequences, she yielded to temptation, and she picked up the yellow one—lemony, lemony bliss. The sweet and tart flavors exploded on her tongue, making her pucker. "Macaroons are coconut cookies."

"I'll take your word for it."

"Chef makes those also." After she wiped her fingers on a napkin, she returned to business. "Everything is on track for tonight."

"And tomorrow's press party?"

"RSVPs are over a hundred people, and we're still fielding requests from influencers. We've got two admins working on clearing their credentials."

A soiree like this was standard fare for a Sterling pre-opening. A number of hosts had gone through a training program to highlight the building's features, including its stunning rooms and suites, residential apartments, world-class spa, salon, and state-of the-art fitness center, complete with a celebrity trainer.

In addition to the La Patisserie, there were six restaurants, an ice-cream parlor, three bars, two boutiques, a gift shop, ample ballrooms for grand events, renowned pieces of art, and even a luxury car showroom. "For tomorrow's Sterling Premier Club offering, we're expecting upward of a thousand attendees." Exclusive sneak peeks of new properties was another of Rafe's ideas. Though there were hundreds of thousands of enrollees in the chain's loyalty program, only the biggest spenders reached premier status. In the industry, his perks were becoming legendary. Guests would be invited to dine and drink at a discount, and they were also encouraged to avail themselves of the swim-up bar and personal cabanas, as well as take advantage of the well-priced spa packages. "We'll be at eighty percent occupancy." Which was extraordinary for a hotel that wouldn't officially open until Friday at noon. "And all the Executive Suites are sold out."

"Excellent."

She went on with her update. "Friday's ribbon cutting will be held at ten a.m. In addition to the economic and city councils along with the visitors' bureau, the mayor has confirmed her attendance. If you can be here no later than nine to greet the dignitaries, that would be ideal."

"You've worked extraordinarily hard on this. Sterling is grateful to you."

Lizzie appreciated his acknowledgment. Her job was consuming every available moment of her life, and because of the long hours, she'd moved into the hotel two weeks prior. It was ridiculous how much she missed Braden, even though they were still in the same city.

Every morning, they had a video call, and they never went to bed without saying good night.

A couple of times, he'd visited her at work, and they'd enjoyed a fine dinner at the hotel's steakhouse before she was called away to deal with a crisis.

He'd arranged to stay after this evening's gathering, but even at that, their limited time together was frustrating. It seemed impossible that he already meant so much to her.

For the first two months after his proposal, she'd kept her small rented house. But she went there less and less frequently. At his urging, she moved her few belongings into his place and had settled in faster than she imagined possible. Ever since she went to work after college, she'd spent almost all of her time on temporary assignments, living in already-furnished rentals. It had been years since she had a real home to come home to, and she loved the peace and comfort of it.

Even though she and Braden rarely discussed it, her upcoming overseas transfer loomed like a dark cloud. She still loved her job and looked forward to the prospect of traveling, but the idea of being away from Braden for weeks or months at a time caused a pit in her stomach.

And there was the challenge of planning their wedding too.

More than once he'd suggested they elope and just throw a big party when they returned. Each day, it was more tempting.

"Elizabeth?"

She shook her head. Rafe had been talking, and she hadn't heard a word. "You were saying?"

"I'm considering creating a new position within the organization."

"Oh?"

"VP of Premier Concierge Services."

She sat up a little taller. He had her complete attention. Every Sterling hotel had highly trained staff who handled special requests. So how was this different?

When Braden asked if he could host his event at the Uptown, Rafe had requested that she personally handle the arrangements. Few things intimidated her, but organizing the private gathering of Titans was one of them. And it wasn't just because of the attendees' demands. She knew how much the evening meant to Braden. He wanted to raise money from the group, and a lot of it.

Julien Bonds, the eccentric and self-proclaimed genius of Silicon Valley, had become interested in movies and was passionate about promenading down the red carpet with his beautiful girlfriend by his side. But the last movie he was involved with hadn't earned a billion dollars at the box office. Furious at the dismal nine hundred million dollars that he labeled an absolute disaster, he'd sent out a rare—

and ill advised—press release stating the action film wouldn't have bombed if he'd retained creative control over the project instead of the bumbling fuckwit who directed it.

The award-winning bumbling fuckwit had taken great offense at the insult.

In the ensuing and highly public row, Bonds decided he needed his own movie studio, and it was Braden's job to bring potential investors to the table. He'd confessed it wouldn't be an easy sell. The genius didn't want to play with his own money. Not only that, but he was willing to offer nothing but vague assurances of massive profits. Still…it was Julien Bonds, and the genius was known for getting people to listen to outrageous ideas.

Rafe went on. "This evening's gathering has highlighted the need for such a special skillset."

Intrigued, she leaned forward.

Coordinating the myriad details for this event had forced her to expand her talents. She'd arranged for private plane and helicopter flights, limousine services, even a security detail. One of the members—Dominic Raul Ricci—required accommodations for an entire entourage, including bodyguards and his right-hand man, booked into the system under the name Davin Sorensen, VP of Special Security. Whatever that meant.

None of tonight's invited guests wanted to be seen in public, so arrangements had been made to bring them into the parking garage through an unmarked entrance where their vehicles would be directed to a special elevator.

The menu was extraordinary, the champagne expensive, the cognac one hundred years old.

"Discretion and understanding the unique needs of VIPs are the key components of the job."

"Of course." Why was he telling her this?

"You're the right person for the position, Elizabeth. And I'd like to offer it to you."

"What?" Stunned, her mind spinning a dozen directions at the implications, she rolled her shoulders back.

"You are uniquely qualified."

"Me? In what way?"

"May I be blunt?"

"Please." She didn't want to be kept guessing.

"Braden has put forth your name for membership consideration in the Titans. You'll be one of us."

Which was presupposing she'd be approved.

"That will carry weight within the membership." His phone rang, but he ignored it, continuing to focus on her and the discussion. "I'm aware you requested an overseas transfer, and I'll see to it that it's expedited if that's your ultimate decision. Your ability to properly manage unique, unusual get-togethers such as this one proves that you—and by extension, Sterling—are the natural choice to host VIP events."

Since Lizzie accepted Braden's proposal, he'd supplied her with more details about the Zeta Society. The organization owned a massive estate in Louisiana, and he'd promised to take her there when her schedule permitted. The annual gathering was held on the premises, along with steering committee meetings and membership inductions. Since the numerous cottages and the mansion with its restaurant, bar, and hotel rooms were open year round, Titans could sequester themselves away in secrecy. But it wasn't always practical for them to make the trek to the retreat on the banks of the Mississippi River.

"As you know, I'd like to expand the Sterling portfolio by offering services for discerning guests."

She nodded.

"They can even be hosted at places that we don't own. For

example, Griffin Lahey has a private island, and he occasionally allows friends and colleagues to stay there."

"He does?"

"That's where I finally managed to convince Hope to marry me. I think it was the sunset. Or the moon. But whatever it was, I'm grateful for it."

Rafe rarely allowed employees glimpses inside his personal life, so it meant a lot to her that he was opening up.

"There are properties all over the world like this. We can match Premier cardholders with locations otherwise unavailable to the public. Perfect for weddings, reunions, annual corporate meetings, private getaways. We can handle all the logistics."

Her eyes widened as she caught his vision. From meetings she'd attended in the past, she knew he'd been moving this direction for years. Currently he was in negotiations with a travel agency to provide destination experiences for thrill-seekers and people looking for unique experiences.

"You've been based in numerous cities throughout the world and know almost all aspects of the service industry."

As he spoke, excitement made Lizzie's heart pick up its pace. "What would be involved?"

"Travel, of course. Some international. Most of it would be within the continental United States. You'd have the opportunity to be in Houston more than you were gone."

Which meant more time with Braden. She took a breath, trying to be professional and not seem overeager. It was as if this job was created just for her, and maybe it had been.

"As VP of the division, you'd report directly to me, and you'd have a suite of offices at corporate headquarters. Of course, you'd be free to hire a staff. You'll need an executive assistant, and I'd leave it to you to present me with a structure for the department, but I imagine you'll want liaisons to work with personnel at all of our properties." He leveled a glance at her. "I meant it when I said you were uniquely qualified for this, Elizabeth."

Lizzie wanted to pinch herself. Braden would be thrilled. Which made her wonder... "Did anyone"—her future spouse?—"suggest this to you?"

"I know what you're asking." His stare was as cold as it was honest. "The answer is no. The idea is mine alone. This is a natural fit with the Sterling Worldwide brand."

She hadn't realized she was holding her breath until it rushed out in a sigh of relief.

"Take some time to think about it," he encouraged. "I can give you a week. After that I'll need to consider other candidates."

If he was planning to move ahead regardless of her decision, then he was serious about his plans. "When would the job start?"

"As soon as possible. Monday."

When she sputtered, he took a drink of his cappuccino. "Or within the month," he amended. "After you've had some time off."

In addition to the annual vacation package that Sterling Worldwide provided, she had accrued half a year of leave to compensate for all the overtime she worked. She'd definitely planned to use some of it next week, beginning on Sunday morning. Braden planned to pick her up at the hotel, then continue on to Galveston, where they'd stay at a resort on the seawall before leaving for a seven-night cruise, and their first trip together. He'd tempted her by offering unlimited rum punches, warm chocolate melting cake, white sandy beaches, and a day at the spa. It would be just the thing she needed to relax and catch up on sleep.

"What are your initial thoughts?"

"It's..." She fished around for the right word. Fabulous. Amazing. She was tempted to leap without thinking about it.

Reminding herself to be a professional businesswoman, she settled for a nondescript word. "Unexpected."

"I imagine it is."

"And the salary?" At present her income was supplemented by the fact that Sterling Worldwide covered her living expenses, and she didn't need a vehicle. When she ate at one of their restaurants, her meals were comped, so it was possible that she'd be essentially earning less overall, even with a raise.

The figure he named was so far beyond what she expected that she scooted farther back in her seat in shock, struggling to keep her lips together so she didn't reveal her excitement.

"Does that meet your approval?"

"It's a good starting place for negotiations." How had she even managed to get that sentence out?

"Indeed." His reply was matter-of-fact, as if he'd expected her to have a counteroffer.

She wanted to discuss the opportunity with Braden before deciding, just as she'd expect him to talk with her about anything that would impact their future. "I'm happy to give you an answer when I'm back at work."

He pulled out his Bonds cell phone. "The Wednesday of your return? Give you a bit to settle in. Ten a.m. in my office?"

"Perfect." Pretending that her fingers weren't shaking, Lizzie entered the appointment into her own calendar.

After closing the calendar app, she stood. "If you will excuse me? As you know, I have an important event to handle this evening."

"Indeed you do. I'll see you there."

They shook hands before she made her way back across the lobby, stopping a couple of times to answer staff questions.

Once she was inside her office, she closed the door and fist-bumped the air. If she had scripted her future, she couldn't have written a better story. She had her very own prince and—very possibly—the job of her dreams. Getting to choose her staff was an added benefit. For years, she'd wanted to work with her friend Crystal, and now the chance might arise.

Her desk phone rang, interrupting her private celebration and reminding her there was still a lot of work to be done.

With a sigh, she pushed back her hair and answered the call.

✑

The evening hadn't yet started, but Braden couldn't fucking wait for it to end so he could take his very sexy fiancée to bed.

While she was away from home, he'd done his best to be supportive, but he missed having her in their bed.

For a man who'd spent so long avoiding relationships, his reaction to living with Lizzie shocked him. It wasn't just easy; it was natural. She was the last piece of the puzzle he needed to complete his life.

He'd hoped for a few stolen moments together before the gathering, and he'd arrived at the hotel early, just in case.

But when he opened the door to their suite, he found she'd sent up a bottle of champagne and a charcuterie board, along with a personal note—a handwritten apology that she couldn't get away and a promise that she would be all his after the event ended.

At least for the majority of the night, she'd be by his side, as his future bride. It was a small consolation.

Braden checked his tie in the bathroom mirror. He had to admit Rafe's hotel was spectacular. The attention to detail made everything at the Uptown five star, and nothing was overstated. The cabinet was teak, and the floating countertop with its double sinks was hewn from gray marble. A bright yellow orchid provided a startling splash of relief.

There was an oversize tile shower with a large soaker tub nearby. Caveman that he was, all Braden could think of was watching Lizzie sink into the depths. That image caused an instant reaction that took some self-discipline to tame.

A minute or two later, when he was ready, he returned to their bedroom to lay several lengths of rope on the duvet cover. Next to them, he placed a red tie—the same one she'd been holding when he discovered her in his closet.

With a satisfied nod, he left the suite and headed toward the elevator.

A hotel employee greeted him the moment he exited the car and directed him to the private dining area with thick etched-glass walls that provided light but didn't allow passersby to see inside.

Immediately the expansive view captured him. The sun was setting, and the taller uptown buildings refracted the light. But the only thing that mattered to him was the sight of Lizzie standing near a window, talking to Rafe.

Her hair was swept into an exquisite updo, and a single tendril curled against her nape. Along with tall, spiky pumps, she wore a sleeveless short black dress that hugged her gorgeous body.

Hunger for her ravaged him, and he strode across the floor. As he drew closer, her body stiffened, as if she sensed his presence; then she slowly turned her head to glance his direction. Their gazes met, and her eyes widened even as her lips parted in sinful invitation. Heat arrowed through him. She was his. *His* woman. And every part of him blazed with the need for everyone to know it.

A moment later, he joined the pair.

"Ah, Braden." Rafe extended his hand.

Only because years of friendship and general good manners demanded it, Braden accepted, but he quickly turned toward Lizzie and brushed his lips against her exposed nape. She might be Rafe's employee, but she was here as Braden's hostess and future wife. "I've missed you," he whispered against her ear.

There was no way she couldn't know how much he desired her, and she blushed. Then, not giving a damn that it was entirely inappropriate, he captured her chin and kissed her delicious mouth.

For a moment, she curled her hand around his wrist, holding on, sealing their connection.

"I love you, Lizzie."

Her smile was for him, and only him, and that knowledge lowered his blood pressure.

Their shared moment was interrupted by a server offering wine. Rafe accepted, but Braden declined, as did Lizzie. Julien Bonds wanted almost a billion dollars from tonight's invitees. Since Braden had brought the heavy-hitters together and paid for the function, he stood to collect a hefty commission.

The gamble might be too risky for some, or all. If that was the case, he'd be out the money he'd fronted.

However, if everything went as well as he hoped, he and Lizzie would have even more to celebrate later with the champagne she'd sent to the suite. For now, he needed to keep his brain clear. Or as clear as it could be when he was drowning in the headiness of her sweet scent.

One thing was certain—in the future, he couldn't go days and days without making love to her. He craved—no, *needed* —his connection with her.

Rafe cleared his throat, interrupting Braden's thoughts. It took effort to refocus on his friend.

"Elizabeth and I were just going over the final details."

"Dinner is at nine, followed by coffee and liqueurs." Lizzie picked up the conversation. "The presentation will begin at ten o'clock. We'll end with a dessert bar."

"The link-up with Bonds has been tested, I presume?" Of course, the elusive Julien had no intention of actually gracing the event with his larger-than-life presence. Instead, he planned to project in, and God only knew how.

Rafe nodded. "Penn himself was here to run a test with Grant."

Though Grant Kingston was vocal about his preference to stay in his private retreat—a cavelike home built into a mountain in New Mexico—he now spent most of his time in California running the Bonds empire so Julien could cultivate new ideas.

Penn—no first name, no last name—was legendary, and one scary motherfucker. He was an associate of Julien's, but even he didn't call the man a friend.

During his years in the military, Penn was highly decorated, renowned for his intelligence as well as his stone-cold bravery. His hue was as dark as the shadows in which he loomed, and he was not an average man. Known as the Equalizer, he stood taller than most, and his smoldering black eyes were the expression of the intensity in his soul.

There was credible evidence that he was under investigation by numerous law enforcement agencies around the world. So far—maybe with the help of Bonds?—no one had been able to make anything stick.

Through various offshore companies, Penn had risked his cash with Braden a number of times, and the amounts had been significant.

Hope, Rafe's fiancée, walked into the room and waved in their direction.

"If you'll excuse me?"

While his friend went to greet her, Braden seized the opportunity to kiss Lizzie again, this time the way he wanted to.

Her tongue danced with his, and she leaned into him to wrap her arms around his neck. She tasted sweet—of promise and the future. No matter how long he lived, he would never get enough of her.

Before he was ready to let her go, she eased away from him, leaving him desperate for more. "I'm thinking of telling Bonds to fuck off and dragging you upstairs."

"You won't." She smiled. "You've got too much at stake."

How well she knew him and understood the risks. But it didn't mean he wasn't tempted.

Hope and Rafe joined them, and Braden was pleased when Hope hugged Lizzie. He liked that his future wife already had a relationship with his best friend's betrothed.

"We have to do lunch," Hope told Lizzie. "Or maybe a girls' night out."

"Not until after I get her back from vacation." He glanced at Rafe. "She has a very demanding boss."

Lizzie's scowl was so fierce it would have scared the hell out of a lesser man.

When she addressed Rafe, her tone was firm. "Braden is speaking on his own behalf. I have no complaints about my job or the hours."

"Rafe's jealous of my time too," Hope said.

Braden bristled. "I'm not—"

The women interrupted in unison. "You are."

Outnumbered, knowing he was beat, he shrugged.

The arrival of a server with a tray of wine for Hope saved him.

Within minutes, Zane Kentwood the entered the room, and Braden excused himself to greet the fellow Titan. Though they might be considered rivals of sorts, Braden admired the man recognized as one of the most aggressive managers at Bradford Capital.

The firm was based on the East Coast and was regarded as one of the top ten hedge funds in the world. Because of his skill and thirst for risk, Kentwood had amassed a stunning fortune of his own, and he was here at Julien's request.

Lizzie joined them, and she greeted Kentwood with genuine warmth. Her confidence, brilliant conversational skills, and uncanny ability to remember names and meaningful details about people had endeared her to his colleagues and friends. She made a hell of a partner in business and in life. Odd to think that just six months ago he wouldn't have believed that was possible.

When Celeste Fallon—as regal as an avenging angel—arrived, electricity zapped across the air. Along with Rafe, she served on the Zeta Society's steering committee. A Fallon had been a founding member back in the 1800s, and ever since then, the family's law and public relations firm had been making problems go away for high-profile clients. She knew everyone's dirtiest little secrets, some of them dating back several generations. When it suited her, she had no qualms about using them to her advantage. Braden liked her. Respected her. Appreciated her services.

"If you'll excuse us?"

"I've wanted to meet you." She studied Lizzie as they shook hands.

"It's my pleasure, ma'am."

"Your name has come before the membership committee."

Lizzie's smile faltered before she caught herself. "I understand there's quite a waitlist."

If Braden were holding a glass, he'd tip it her direction. Her nonanswer was perfect. She didn't fawn or ask if Celeste knew the status, which undoubtedly she did. Nothing happened in the organization without Celeste being aware of it.

While Hope wandered over to say hello to Celeste, Rafe greeted Kentwood. The small gathering was almost complete and couldn't be going any better. Kentwood was sipping cognac, and Celeste passed on wine in favor of champagne. But the alcohol was doing its job, allowing conversation to flow.

Next to arrive was Kian Brannigan. Since they hadn't been in contact for over a year, Braden was surprised when the RSVP arrived. As usual, Kian wore a casual jacket. He'd skipped a tie, and he'd left a couple of buttons open on his shirt. His face bore several days' growth, and his hair looked as if it only had a passing acquaintance with a brush.

Presumably from working on his motorcycle, the knuckles of his tattooed hands sported several fresh cuts.

When offered a glass of wine, he asked for something stronger. "Whiskey?"

"Of course, sir. Any particular brand?"

Kian named a single malt. "Make it a double."

When they were alone, he studied the man that no one knew well. "How are you doing?"

"Had a lead a couple of weeks ago."

The hollowness in Kian's response matched the flatness in his eyes, telling Braden all he needed to know.

Though his only sibling had been born premature and passed shortly thereafter, he couldn't begin to understand the living hell that was Kian's life. When he was young, he lost his parents and little sister in a plane crash. While the bodies of his mother, father, and the pilot had been recovered, Sara had never been found.

After the tragedy, Kian had run away often and gotten into trouble, and God knew where he'd have ended up without his uncle, not that the man was any type of good influence.

Everything Kian did was focused around his never-ending quest to find out what happened to Sara.

"Fuck." The drink arrived, and he downed it in a single gulp.

Braden signaled to the server for another.

Just then, Hope wandered over to say hello. Her smile was warm, and Kian responded in kind, the first positive emotion Branden ever remembered seeing from the haunted man.

About five minutes before nine, Braden excused himself to greet Dominic Ricci and his right-hand man. While Braden and the other gentlemen were in sports coats, Ricci and Sorensen wore bespoke suits. Dominic, with his square jaw and his hair raked back from his forehead, projected an aura of danger and invincibility, suitable for his place among the most respected—and feared—men in the Texas business world.

At the top of the hour, Lizzie let people know that dinner was being served. Since Penn still hadn't arrived, Braden sent him a text message.

Once everyone else was in the space reserved for the meal, he followed. The guests were finding their place cards and taking their seats at the round table. That had been one of his few contributions to the planning sessions. At an event with people accustomed to commanding the utmost respect, he didn't want any seat to seem more important than another.

Servers offered wine, and Penn's empty chair was obvious.

Two magnificent iced seafood towers were already in place when the man arrived. The air chilled, and talking ceased. Penn swept his gaze over the gathered people before acknowledging Rafe.

Braden stood to greet the late arrival, who wore aviator sunglasses, a leather bomber jacket, black jeans, and a ball cap bearing the Bonds logo. Tonight, instead of running shoes, he wore boots. With their battle scars, they were serviceable rather than dressy. "Glad you're here."

The man's handshake was firm and strong, and Braden had no doubt there was restraint behind it.

When he spoke, Penn's deep voice was emotionless. "Bonds has his ways."

"Indeed." Which was why Braden had been convinced to assemble this group of individuals.

Penn removed his hat from his clean-shaven head and tucked the bill in his back pocket. Then he took off his glasses and slid them inside his jacket. In the year or so since Braden last saw the other man, the lines between his eyebrows had become deeper entrenched. Though it shouldn't be possible, the faint scar on his cheekbone seemed even longer, more jagged.

Lizzie joined them. "Hello, Penn."

"Elizabeth." He took her hand, and his grip was loose, gentle, nothing like the one he'd used with Braden.

Lizzie knew the man? "The fuck?" Braden slid a possessive arm around her waist.

"Easy." Penn released Elizabeth, then grinned, knocking a decade off his face. "Nothing to worry about. I met Elizabeth this afternoon when we were doing the AV check."

That his sweet, innocent Lizzie didn't actually know the Equalizer was a small comfort.

"The royal red shrimp are divine." Lizzie was the consummate hostess, and for that Braden was grateful. Then she went on, as if he didn't have a tight grip on her. "Have you tried them?"

Penn shook his head.

"They taste a bit like lobster. I think you'll enjoy them."

Trust her to smooth the situation.

The threesome returned to the table, and Braden performed introductions. It was only a minute later, when Lizzie placed her hand on his thigh, that he relaxed.

Her touch reassured him and strengthened their bond. What the ever-living hell was wrong with him, anyway? He'd never experienced even a hint of jealousy in any other relationship. So it didn't make sense now. She wore his ring and met his carnal desires with ones of her own. One thing was sure—he couldn't punch the living shit out of every man she came in contact with.

As the main course was served, Rafe asked Penn a question, and Braden relaxed.

The camaraderie he'd been hoping to foster developed as the meal progressed. By the time Lizzie mentioned that a dessert bar would open after the presentation, people had angled their chairs in order to engage in deep discussions.

He couldn't hope for a better atmosphere when asking people for a shitpile of money that might vanish into celluloid history.

A symphonic explosion of sound rocked the space, and steam billowed from all corners and the overhead vents.

Braden swung his gaze from Rafe to Penn. "What the fuck?"

*"A genius is trying to reach you."*

"That would be Bonds." Penn's words were somewhat unnecessary.

"I'm as surprised as you are." Rafe shook his head. "I wasn't invited to the test run."

Penn lifted one shoulder. "The music? That's his theme song."

"You're serious?" What kind of person had their own actual score?

As the decibels lowered to slightly less than hearing

damaging, a shimmering 3D Bonds figure appeared at the edge of the table. He was dressed—or rather the image was—in a tuxedo with tails. In typical Bonds fashion, the bow tie wasn't black. Instead, he'd opted for some sort of bizarre color. In addition, the loops were limp and different sizes. Did the man own a mirror? A top hat was perched cockily on his head. He held a vaudeville-like cane, which he brandished about like a sword.

"A mixed metaphor." Penn reached for his coffee. "But I like it."

Then as everyone watched, rapt with shock and awe, the image tap-danced.

Lizzie leaned toward Braden and whispered against his ear. "I love his athletic shoes."

"They're"—Braden blinked at the neon-bright atrocities—"purple."

"More like violet. They coordinate with his bow tie."

"They do?"

Still tapping—and how was it possible for sneakers to make that sound?—Julien, or his apparition, moved to a platform in the middle of the table. Platform? More like a stage, complete with steps for him to ascend.

By the time he was in place, the center of attention, the music cut off, making the sudden silence shocking. Braden's ears were ringing.

"Felicitations, one and all." Julien looked directly at Braden. "Thank you for putting this together."

At first, Braden thought Julien's hologram was preprogrammed, but he was interacting as if he were actually in the room.

"And I adore your future wife. Very competent." The image turned a bit, and he blew a kiss toward Lizzie. "Thank you. If you're ever looking for a job—"

"She's not." Rafe's interruption was met by a round of laughs.

"The offer stands. And you, Rafe… Your hotel is stupendous. Makes me want to travel to Texas."

"Obviously not enough to actually get you out of Silicon Valley."

He ignored the comment entirely and moved on. "Hope, my love. Beautiful as ever. I have someone in need of your matchmaking services." He shuddered. "Even with my remarkable talents, I've failed spectacularly. He's about to drive me mad with his maudlin ways. Bothersome, really."

Julien went on, greeting Celeste, Kian, Zane, Dominic, and Devin. Very smart, since Bonds wanted more than a hundred million dollars from each potential investor, but couldn't even get on a plane to join them in person. He ended by thanking Penn for his help. "May I direct your attention… here." He pointed to the front wall with his cane, which had somehow morphed into a light saber.

Then, a movie began to play. It only took a few seconds to realize this was the film that had made Julien livid.

Though Braden had expected Julien's presentation to be unusual, this was beyond anything he'd believed possible.

"Awful. Terrible. Vile." Bonds waved the saber wildly. "Amateur hour. A gaggle of giraffes could have done better!"

To Braden, the special effects appeared stunning. But Penn was nodding as Bonds spoke.

Minutes later, the film froze on an image of a car flying across a ravine.

"This is a travesty of filmmaking. Look at this. An embarrassment among embarrassments. An insult to my poor eyes. Tragic."

Braden glanced at the other guests. From their frowns, he gathered they were as perplexed by this as he was.

"If people weren't insipidly stupidly uninspired, willing to settle for technology six months old, this, this—this!—is what the scene would look like." He shivered as the movie started over.

Even though Braden didn't know specifically what to watch for, the differences were subtle but profound. The colors were crisper, the images sharper, with more depth, almost as if they were viewing in 3D, but without needing glasses. The sound bounced off the walls, shaking Braden's chair.

The film froze in exactly the same place

"Genius. Absolutely genius. Am I right?"

The lights came up, and Braden hadn't even been consciously aware that they'd been lowered.

As if it were a living thing, enthusiasm rippled through the atmosphere.

"And now each of you have the opportunity to be part of something spectacular. This."

Though Braden had prepped everyone in advance, Julien made his announcement as if no one knew what was going on.

"Genius Works is my new company, and we'll be making the best movies, with the best technology on the planet. Together, you and I—or is it you and me? Well, us, all of us— will dazzle the world. Red carpets!" He brandished his saber, the light now the same shade of green as money, and Braden pulled back when the thing got too close.

Then he shook his head. The thing was an illusion, but it had seemed real enough to zap him.

"Trophies."

"Awards?" Penn asked.

"As long as they're gold!" Bonds preened. "And we will have more releases than anyone. Move fast. Hire the best talent. Big productions, small ones. And, and..." He looked into the distance. "Our own streaming service?"

Zane Kentwood, in his bold yet practical way, spoke up. "A step at a time, Bonds."

"Yes. Yes. So...how much can I count on you for?"

"You interested in Bradford Capital funds?"

"No. This is a private endeavor. For..." He paused. "Brilliant strategists."

"Meaning you don't want to answer to anyone but yourself."

"Well, I wouldn't put it *quite* that way."

Zane waited.

"Fine." He huffed. "I'm tired of small minds." Then he doffed his hat. "Which you clearly are not. I'm correct, am I not?"

Everyone turned in his direction.

To his credit, Kentwood relaxed against his seatback. "Flattery doesn't work. I'm interested in a minority stake in the venture."

"Proved your brilliance! Thank you, sir. And to you next, Kian."

"I can see some value. I want to have a show produced about the plane crash. Or something that can go on one of the new channels."

Bonds nodded. "Reasonable request. Even a new docuseries, perhaps? With a consistent narrator?"

"Make it happen, and I'll make arrangements with Braden."

"Thank you. And the incomparable Celeste?"

"Nice dinner. Impressive presentation, as expected." She was as steely as she was unflappable. "I understand you haven't switched your PR firm yet."

"How remiss." He turned away for a moment. "Aria..."

Braden had met Aria, Julien's CEE, Chief Executive of Everything. Of course, outside of his organization, a CEE didn't exist.

"Can you make this problem go away? Throw some meat to the hungry lion, as it were?"

Penn cleared his throat. "Hot mic, Bonds."

Lizzie looked at him, and he shrugged. There was no way Bonds didn't know he was still broadcasting.

"Ah. Was it?" He looked back at Celeste and performed a flourishing bow. "Apologies, Celeste."

"Once you've resolved this...oversight, I'll be in touch with Braden."

At that moment, her cell phone lit up. *"A genius is trying to reach you."*

"And there you are. Problem solved. You can have that conversation straightaway. Before you leave, even. Save you some time and bother. You're welcome." With a self-congratulatory grin, he turned toward Dominic.

Braden marveled at Julien's approach. People with this kind of ask didn't generally put each person on the spot. Then again, no one else was Bonds.

It took another thirty minutes for him to finish going around the room. When Julien was finished, Braden had no doubt the invitees would offer up every penny of the billion dollars. Even he intended to write a check. Though he had no desire to accumulate awards, it was thrilling to be on the forefront of technological and creative advances. With Bonds at the helm, the movie studio adventure would either be a massive success or a devastating failure.

"Don't dally-dilly. Offer expires at midnight tomorrow." With that, his image disintegrated, becoming a million fractured stars before twinkling away into nothingness.

For a long moment, no one said a word.

Then Lizzie stood. "The dessert bar is open in the prefunction area. We also have espresso drinks, as well as champagne for celebrating." She motioned toward a member of the hotel staff, and the doors opened.

He marveled at her. She'd done a spectacular job this evening, better than he could have ever hoped for.

Now that the aftereffects of Julien's visual illusion wore off, talking resumed, and the guests began to move toward the anteroom.

Lizzie chatted with each person before ordering a cappuccino.

Braden surveyed the extravagant dessert selections. Cakes, brownies, chocolates, gelatos, and tiny bright things that appeared to be some sort of cookies.

Rafe and Hope approached, and she selected a couple of chocolates.

"Stick with something recognizable." Rafe tossed a disdainful look toward the display. "Those things taste like a tree."

Lizzie joined them. "Rafe is talking about the purple macarons. They're actually floral. Lavender and rose."

"Just think, Hope. We can grow stuff in our yard for chef to use in the kitchen."

"I have to try one." Hope added one to her plate, then took a tiny test bite. "Oh, my taste buds just fell in love." She finished it off before choosing another.

Rafe gave her a quizzical look.

"What? It's fabulous. I'm going to want these at my next meet-and-greet."

Braden and Lizzie excused themselves to mingle. He had funds to secure, and probably dozens of questions to answer.

"I wanted to tell you something." Lizzie placed her unfinished coffee on a tray as they walked away.

"Oh?"

"I'm not wearing panties."

Heat raced through him, and he almost tripped over his own feet before catching her wrist. "Do you know how dangerous that information is?"

She smiled, at once angelic and devilish. "I hope to find out after we finish making our rounds."

Which she'd just made ten times more difficult.

"Where shall we start?"

He took a quick glance around. Dominic and his right-hand man were sipping liqueur near the window. Celeste held a glass of champagne and was holding court with Zane and Kian. Penn had vanished.

*Interesting.*

"I've got an idea of my own." Since no one was paying attention to them, he placed his hand on the small of her back and guided her back into the dining room.

"We can't do this!"

"Oh yes. We most assuredly can." To be safe, since she was well-known at the hotel, he pulled her behind a tall potted plant.

"This is getting to be a habit."

His grin was quick and hungry. "It will be." He cradled the back of her head with one hand and slid the other up her right thigh and beneath the hem of her skirt to cup her buttock.

"Braden—"

With barely restrained passion, he claimed her mouth.

His Lizzie.

Her gentle sigh and sweet response nourished him. She was light where there'd only been darkness. Hope where there had been despair.

Wanting more, he deepened the kiss as he moved his hand, seeking out her pussy. She was wet and ready for him.

Braden dipped two fingers inside her, making her moan, weakening her knees so that she grabbed hold of him for support.

The kiss went on and on as she gave him everything he asked for.

A full minute later, when they were both breathless, he slowly let her go and straightened her dress. "Don't clean up. I want your thighs sticky so that you can't stop thinking about me."

"Yes." Through her long eyelashes, she looked up at him. "Sir."

Until Lizzie, he'd had no idea just how much he liked the sound of that word.

As she watched, he brought his fingers to his mouth and sucked her essence off them. "You complete me, woman."

"I love you, Braden."

He never tired of hearing those words. A hundred times a day would never be enough.

"You need to get back out there and close some deals."

She was right, but that didn't mean he still didn't want to devour her right here, right this moment.

He settled for tipping her chin back, claiming her mouth one more time to let her taste herself on his tongue.

Lizzie's soft moan fed something deep inside him. "Braden…"

"Yeah. I know." He tucked a wayward strand of her hair behind her ear. The intimate exchange they'd just shared would have to hold him until he could get rid of everyone. At least he fucking hoped he could make it through the next hour or so without abandoning his guests and dragging her back to their suite.

∽

Braden closed the hotel door behind them and set the privacy lock, slamming Lizzie's heart into overdrive.

"I've been losing my mind all night." He advanced toward her, but she stayed in place, riveted by the intent brewing in his eyes—more gray than normal. Over the months they'd been together, she'd learned to recognize the color. During everyday events, they had a greener hue. But when he was aroused, steely determination radiated from them. He intended to have her tonight, and nothing would stop him.

She was desperate for him too. Sex with him was amazing, but it was more than that. It gave her a sense of belonging and comfort.

"I don't want to be apart for this long ever again."

"Me either." A good-morning kiss and a few minutes together over a cup of coffee ensured her entire day went better. The knowledge that she'd be in his arms when she finished work gave her something to look forward to. "About that…"

"Yes?"

"Rafe has offered me a new position." She hadn't meant to bring this up until tomorrow, but the timing was right.

"Oh?"

"Do you mind if we sit down?"

"Will it keep you away from me for longer periods of time? If so, I may have to kill him."

"I would have refused immediately if that was the case." She smiled. "In fact it's just the opposite. I was struggling with the idea of leaving you for that overseas assignment."

As they walked toward the comfortable couch, he threaded his fingers with hers in a gesture that was as natural as it was intimate. "Champagne? My thoughtful fiancée sent up a rather nice bottle."

"I'd love some. Thank you. And you have a lot to celebrate tonight."

"It would not have been as perfect without your help." He popped the cork, then filled two flutes.

They clinked the rims together before he sat next to her, close enough that his pheromones threatened to derail her thoughts. "Congratulations, Mr. Gallagher. I think you may have raised that billion dollars tonight."

"It's close. We may need to do one more event to put us over the top."

She took a tiny sip, and the bubbles tickled her nose. "I've got to admit I've never been part of anything quite like that. Julien is more than I imagined." And she'd heard rumors about him for years.

"He doesn't play by anyone's rules."

"But those effects? Seriously? The wineglasses on the table were shaking. And the image... What was it, anyway?"

Braden relaxed back, crossing his legs at the ankles. "Your guess is as good as mine. Some sort of hologram? But I didn't think technology had advanced that far."

"I would have said it was a projection, but it interacted with people and had real-time reactions."

"Which is what makes him a genius."

"You're investing?"

"I am. But we should discuss the amount."

Cocking her head to the side, she studied him. "Why?"

"Why? It's a lot of money with a massive potential upside. Even at that, return on investment will take years. And with Hollywood, there are no guarantees. It might be like setting a pile of cash on fire. Since we're going to be married—"

"I appreciate that. But really, it's your money."

His correction was swift and firm. "Ours."

"Braden, really—" At his furious scowl, she broke off. She had a small savings account, and since they'd been together, he hadn't allowed her to pay for anything. "Even if you lose the house, we can stay together at one of Rafe's properties." After another drink, the alcohol warmed her insides. That was more than enough, especially since Braden no doubt had plans for her. "Perk of the job."

"Pass. I'd never risk your future."

Lizzie adored how protective he was, and she scooted a tiny bit closer to him. "Then the choice is yours." She slid her glass onto the coffee table. "Is it terrible of me to admit I might actually want to walk the red carpet at least once?"

"I'll be honored to be your date."

No doubt Crystal would love to go dress shopping together.

"Now tell me about your job offer."

She angled her body so she could look into his eyes. Then she forgot what she was going to say. She was lost in him, even though they'd been together for months.

Braden traced a random pattern on her thigh.

"Now I'll never remember what we were talking about."

"The new position?"

Maybe she should have waited for the morning to mention it. The longing inside her was bigger than almost anything.

"Lizzie?"

For a moment, she closed her eyes. Then when she opened them, she captured his wrist. "You have to stop that."

"What?" He raised his eyebrows, pretending innocence.

She moved his hand to his thigh. "Keep it there."

"You're sexy when you're bossy."

Then she couldn't help it; she smiled in unison with him.

No other relationship had ever been like this. Sometimes she wanted to pinch herself to be sure it was real. "So...it would be VP of Premier Concierge Services division."

"Oh?" All traces of teasing vanished from his tone as well as his face.

"It's a new position." With enthusiasm, she outlined the responsibilities.

"You did a hell of a job for me tonight."

"Rafe is always thinking about ways to take hospitality

offerings to a new level. There's a niche market for high-end experiences and gatherings."

"I admire his astuteness in asking you."

She knew it was more than flattery. He meant what he was saying. "It involves a pay raise, and I'd be based in Houston. Of course I'd have to travel occasionally, but I can't imagine I'd be gone more than a week at a time." Which was better than months.

"What are you thinking? Are you considering it?" His words were a bit flat, hedged in caution.

"As you said earlier, we're getting married. I wanted to get your opinion before giving him an answer."

"Lizzie." He placed his glass next to hers before turning to her. "I'd never ask you to give up your career aspirations. You've worked too damn hard and long to get where you are. I'll follow you to the ends of the earth to be with you."

How was it possible to be even more in love with him now than she had been five minutes ago?

"If you want to go overseas, I'll pack my bags. Make whatever choice is best for you and your career. We'll make it work, no matter what."

Beyond happy, she wrapped her arms around herself. "I don't have to give him an answer until we get back from the cruise. But I think I'm going to say yes. I love our life together here." And she would get to spend more time with her family that way.

Her mother was now only working one day a week for them, and in a much different role. Now she was the household manager, and she'd hired a chef who did meal preparation three nights a week. But in typical Eileen fashion, she still kept the cookie jar filled.

She had the opportunity to become a nanny to Sandra's baby, a job she loved, and one she said she was keeping until Lizzie and Braden had their own children.

That comment had sucked the breath from Lizzie. But Braden had nodded and commented that he hoped it was sooner, rather than later.

"Always, Lizzie, your happiness is my priority."

Almost always, he initiated their kisses. This time, she did.

She moved to her knees, then straddled him and placed her hands on his shoulders. "Do you know how much I appreciate you?"

"Can't be even half as much as I appreciate you. You were fucking amazing back there. I'm so proud that you're mine."

Lizzie feathered her hands into his gloriously thick hair. The steel in his eyes turned molten.

His mouth was hot, and their kiss seared her. She still tasted herself on his tongue, even though that shouldn't be possible.

He placed his hands on her waist to bring her forward, and his cock pressed against her. Response flooded her, and she ground her hips against him.

*"Fuck."* With a groan, he pulled back to imprison her hands and lower them to her sides. "Before we get too carried away, I have plans for you."

A strange combination of excitement and nerves sent her brain into a freefall.

"I can't believe I'm stopping you." He slid her off his lap. "Come with me." After standing, he assisted her up.

He crossed to the window to close the blinds.

"You know you don't have to."

"I have an aversion to anyone but me seeing you naked."

"Believe me. You're the only man I want looking at me."

He pushed the privacy button, lowering the blackout screen.

"No one can see in these windows. There was an incident at a hotel near the Denver airport. After a shower, a guest was walking around with no clothes. A woman in another tower saw him and called the police. The poor guy got ticketed for indecent exposure and had to go to court. So all of Rafe's properties protect his guests—and the unsuspecting public—from such unfortunate events."

"In that case…" He crooked his finger.

Unhesitatingly she went to him.

In a smooth, practiced move, he pulled her dress up, then off.

"Christ, Lizzie." He dropped the garment on a nearby chair. "That you weren't wearing panties killed me. But no bra either?"

With a grin, she loosened the knot in his tie. "I told you I missed you."

He captured her breasts, then rolled her nipples between his thumbs and forefingers.

Response flooded her, and she moaned.

It took him only a few seconds to undress, but it seemed like an eternity.

Even though she knew every muscle and sinew of him, his hard, lean form captivated her.

His cock jutted toward her, and she reached to curl her hand around the impressive girth.

Braden placed his hand on hers as he shook his head. "I've got to be inside you."

Galvanized by the tone in his voice and the set of his jaw, she hurried toward the bed, only to freeze at the foot of it.

White rope lay there, along with the red tie that was the center of so many of her fantasies. Back then, it had been impossible to believe that the city's renowned scandalous billionaire would fall in love with her. Lizzie glanced back at him. "You remembered."

"Every word you've uttered. Every fantasy you've shared."

He closed the distance between them, making her ache with need. "Stay where you are."

The request surprised her, but she didn't argue. Instead, she watched, fascinated as he picked up one of the strands of rope.

"Please place your hands over your head. Cross your wrists and lace your fingers."

Her pulse slowed as she slowly slipped into an alternate universe, one where no one existed other than Braden and the pleasure he brought her.

His motions were deft as he secured her. Then he gently helped her to sit on the edge of the mattress. "Now I want you on your back."

Because her movements were restricted, obeying was a challenge, but once he had her where he requested, he instructed her to part her legs as wide as she could.

He crossed the room and pulled a chrome spreader bar from his bag. Her rush of nerves receded when she realized it wasn't very long, meaning her legs wouldn't be too far apart.

But he depressed buttons on both ends. She gulped as the wicked thing expanded at least another foot. When would she learn not to underestimate him?

He tapped the insides of her thighs, indicating he wanted them farther apart.

She wriggled from the slight discomfort, arching her back as she tried to find a different position.

"I like watching you writhe. Your nipples are getting even harder. They do that, you know, when you're in bondage with no hope of escape." As he spoke, he crouched and tied her ankles to unyielding hooks.

Even though her struggles were futile, she tugged against the bonds.

"Glorious."

"Should I eat your pussy? Finger-fuck you?"

From his light tone, she knew he wasn't asking her opinion. He knew exactly what he was going to do. Instead, he wanted to torment her. And it was working.

"Perhaps both. But first the flogger."

"On my *front?*"

"I'd blindfold you, but I want you to watch."

She pressed her lips together to smother her instinctive whimper.

Braden returned to the bag to fetch her favorite flogger. It could sting, but it wasn't anything like the heavy leather one they'd recently progressed to.

"How are the bonds?"

"Fine." *Amazing.* The texture was exactly what she imagined. Silky and sensuous, but at the same time strong. A totally different experience than cuffs.

With exquisitely gentle flicks, he covered her chest, breasts, nipples, rib cage, belly, and pelvis with suede caresses. Then he leaned over to kiss away any sting, driving her mad. He trailed his mouth lower and licked between her labia, just long enough to drive her to the edge of an orgasm.

"Braden, I—"

He pulled away to spank her pussy.

The sensation overwhelmed her, making her needier. "I need…" What? "Harder. Please."

Instead of giving her what she wanted, he parted her pussy lips and ate her completely. She jerked helplessly, wanting to grab hold of him and press against his head.

Before she was ready, he moved away.

"That's mean."

"Is that a complaint, sub?"

"Ah…" She thought. Fast. "No. Not at all, Sir."

"I thought not." With zero sympathy he picked up the flogger again.

This time he wielded it with a little more force, a few of the licks making her sob.

"I love your sounds. The louder, the better. Keep watching, Lizzie." With a figure-eight motion, he blazed the insides of her thighs before catching her swollen pussy.

Though an ache ripped through her, she arched up, begging for more, praying he wouldn't stop.

He tossed the implement aside to slide two fingers inside her, parting her wide, seeking and finding her G-spot as he covered her pussy with his mouth.

Screaming his name, Lizzie climaxed, spiraling into a kaleidoscope of bliss. She stayed there, floating, hardly noticing that her legs were no longer spread so far apart.

When she finally blinked the world back into focus, Braden was sitting next to her, rubbing her wrists.

"Welcome back." He smiled at her.

Lizzie struggled to sit up, but she didn't have enough energy.

"I've got you." He gathered her close, offering his body as the warmth and support she needed.

For a few more seconds, she gave herself over to the drowsiness, drifting off again.

When she finally recovered, he moved her to the pillows, then uncapped a water bottle that was on a nightstand. "Have some of this."

She took a small drink before handing it back. "That was… I, uhm…liked what we did."

"I'm planning to bring our toys on the trip. We'll have lots of time to explore and enjoy." He put the bottle back in its place.

"You're going to make love to me?" She stroked his still-hard cock.

"All night, and into tomorrow."

As she expected, he took charge, playing with her pussy

for a moment to ensure she was ready for him before tucking her beneath his strong body and sinking his cock deep inside her.

To Lizzie, there was nothing like this. Being with him completed her.

She met each of his thrusts, reveled in his constant words of love.

Amazing lover that he was, he gave her orgasm after orgasm before seeking his own release.

His breathing became more ragged, and his cock seemed impossibly big. She wrapped her arms around his back, digging in her fingertips.

Then, before he came, he issued a command. "Kiss me."

With everything she had to offer, she did. He took it and asked for more, staking his claim.

"I'll never let you go." With a groan from deep inside and a loud "fuck," he ejaculated, filling her with his hot seed.

Braden was immobilized for several seconds before he shook his head. "Shit. I'm crushing you."

"No." He wasn't. If she had her way, he'd stay there for a long time, allowing her to hold him.

With a long drawn-in breath, he rolled to the side. Instantly he reached for her and tugged her close.

They stayed there, breathing together for a long time. Eventually he twirled a finger into her hair. "Ready for round two?"

"What?" She pushed up onto her elbow. "You can't be serious!"

"Do you know how long it's been since we made love?"

"Less than two minutes."

He grinned and smacked her ass.

"Ouch!" Lizzie swatted his hand away.

"You know what I mean."

"A few days?"

"Which means I have time to make up for." He sat up. "But I'm a kind and generous Dom. I'll give you a few more minutes to recover."

"Very kind. Very generous. The best, even."

He left the bed, and when he returned he was carrying a warm, damp washcloth and their champagne.

After he bathed her, he offered her one of the flutes. "To our future."

She smiled and angled her glass in his direction. "It looks pretty bright, doesn't it?"

"Any chance of an elopement?"

For the first time, she wasn't as against the idea. "We can talk about it."

He whooped. "I won!"

With a laugh, she shook her head. "Hold up! I didn't agree." *Yet.* "Your victory lap is a little premature, Sir."

"I'll take whatever I can get and work on getting to yes." He plucked her untouched drink from her hand and set it aside before nuzzling the side of her neck. "And I think I'll get started on that fabulous future right now…"

◊ ◊ ◊ ◊ ◊

Thank you for reading Scandalous Billionaire! I hope you enjoyed reading Lizzie and Braden's story as much as I loved writing it. I also hope you had fun catching up with old friends and meeting some new book boyfriends.

I invite you to read more about the fascinating and powerful world of the Titans today with a scorching enemies-to-lovers story. Quinn men have been kidnapping O'Malley women for nearly a millennia. And Jack Quinn is no different. He'll do anything to have Sinead as his.

## DISCOVER DETERMINED BILLIONAIRE

For incredibly sexy stories that feature Dominant billionaire alphas, please join me in a visit to the Quarter, New Orleans's exclusive dungeon… His to Claim

It was only supposed to be a weekend fling… After a broken heart, Hannah Mills vowed never to offer more than her body to any Dom, but when she volunteers to be the prize at a slave auction benefiting charity, mysterious philanthropist and notorious playboy Mason Sullivan turns her world inside out…

★★★★★ Full of real, raw, beautiful emotions with vibrant characters. ~*Amazon Reviewer*

## DISCOVER HIS TO CLAIM

To find out more about Mason and Hope, order Billionaire's Matchmaker today! He needs a marriage of convenience. But he doesn't want just any woman. He wants her…the woman hired to find him a bride.

Turn the page for an exciting excerpt from BILLIONAIRE'S MATCHMAKER.

# BILLIONAIRE'S MATCHMAKER EXCERPT

Hope Malloy, his matchmaker, projected competence, but her heels and fanciful handbag gave her a feminine air. A sane man would think of her as a vendor or business associate, so he could slot her into the *off-limits* part of his conscience. She wasn't a potential date or wife. Or submissive.

He wanted her.

*She isn't mine.*

Fuck his conscience.

Before this ridiculous idea about finding him a woman to marry went any further, she needed to know the truth about him, the side he locked away and kept hidden unless he was at one of his favorite BDSM clubs, the side that Celeste should have informed his matchmaker about.

Bare inches separated him from Hope, and he halved that distance by leaning toward her. "Is there a place on your fourteen-page questionnaire to discuss sexual proclivities?"

"I'm not sure what you mean." Her knuckles whitened on her purse strap.

"Let me clarify." Rafe spoke softly into the thick air

between them. "Kinks. Those nasty, scandalous things that people do in the privacy of their own homes. Things they don't talk about in public. Salacious acts that make them drop to their knees in church as they beg forgiveness. Would you consider that compatibility or chemistry?"

Tension tightened her shoulders. "Is there something…" Her tone suggested she was trying for professionalism, but her voice cracked on a sharp inhalation.

After a few more shallow breaths, she ventured, "What do I need to know?"

"I'm into BDSM."

Her beautiful, pouty mouth parted a little.

An image scorched him—that of him slipping a spider gag between her lips, spreading her mouth and keeping it that way. He'd force her to communicate with her expression and her body, like she was now. "Your eyes are wide, Ms. Malloy. Are you shocked? Interested?" Her soul was reflected in the startling depths. "Curious, perhaps?"

It took her less than three seconds to close her mouth and regroup. "No. I'm wondering how I should phrase this for your candidates."

She'd lied. Instead of meeting his gaze, she stared at the potted plant near the window.

Rather than unleashing the beast that suddenly wanted to dominate her, he kept his tone even. "I'm sure you've had clients who like that sort of thing?"

Finally, after a breath, she looked at him. "I'll make some discreet inquiries of the candidates. What is it you're looking for?"

He ached to capture her chin and force her to look at him. "How much do you know about BDSM?"

She pulled back her shoulders, as if on more stable ground. "I've heard of it."

"No personal experience?"

"That's not relevant."

Damn her dishonest answer. Some? None? Would he be her first? Could he take her, mold her into what he wanted?

What the fuck was wrong with him? He'd already decided she was off-limits. "There are as many ways to practice BDSM as there are people in the lifestyle. No relationship is the same."

"Makes sense."

Mesmerized, he watched the wild flutter of her pulse in her throat. It was like oxygen to a dying man. He wanted more. "Some people prefer to confine their practices to the bedroom—at night, for example. Others, on occasion, indulge at a club or play party. A number of people practice it in varying degrees on a twenty-four-hour basis."

"Where do your...proclivities lie?"

Until now, he hadn't considered he might want a submissive wife. Over the years, he'd found it easier to go to the club. He was a Dom who would give a sub what she wanted.

But he'd never allowed himself to think of having a wife that he could call with a list of sensuous instruction. Now, however, with Hope standing there, he couldn't banish the thought. And since his mother had already squandered a hundred grand on the woman's matchmaking services, he figured he should be specific in his requests. More, he wanted Hope to know what she was getting into, even if she didn't yet realize he'd chosen her. "I want my wife to be submissive twenty-four hours a day."

"Can you clarify what you mean?" She clenched the handle of her kitty bag, seeming to pretend this was an ordinary conversation with a normal man.

Rafe captured Hope's shoulders and pulled her into his office so he could close the door. He held on to her for a whole lot longer than was necessary but not as long as he wanted to. How would she react if he eased his first finger up the delicate column of her throat?

Would she surrender? Fight the inevitable?

Forcing himself to resist the driving impulse, he dropped his hands and curled them into fists at his sides.

"Proclivities," she prompted.

The word echoed in his head. "She'll wear a collar—my collar…" And because he could no longer resist, he traced an index finger across the hollow of her throat. Her pulse fluttered, and her breaths momentarily ceased. "My woman will know that she belongs to me and she will behave as such."

Hope's gaze remained locked on his. When she spoke, her voice wobbled. "And this…collar. She'll have to wear it all the time?"

"That's what twenty-four seven means." A devilish grin tugged at his lips. He kept his fingertip pressed to her warm skin. "It will be subtle, however. Nothing gaudy. Unless people knew, I doubt they'd think she was wearing anything other than a striking piece of jewelry. But her play collar, the one she wears in private with me or at a lifestyle event, may be different."

"Like at a BDSM club or something?" She nodded, as if she were on ground she understood.

Not that he'd let her stay there long. "I enjoy showing off my sub. There's a certain restaurant in New Orleans, Vieille Rivière, that she will go to. And a club in the city, also. She will also be expected to join me when I visit people in similar social circles." *Including other Titans.* But there was a limit to how much he should tell her. "There are certain things I would want her to go along with. Bondage. Sensory deprivation."

"You mean like blindfolds and handcuffs?" There was no hesitation in her words, so he ascertained she'd made sense of what he'd said and decided that fell under the category of typical bedroom shenanigans.

"Among others, yes. I use blindfolds on occasion. I like gags so that my woman must beg with her eyes. Her tears are like dripping nectar from the gods."

Wide-eyed, uncertain, she sucked in a deep, disbelieving breath.

"I will want to her to wait for me at the end of a long day, on her knees, head tipped back, her beautiful mouth open for me." He pictured her naked in front of the door, hungry for his touch.

She retreated a step. "Mr. Sterling, I—"

"My wife will focus on me and my pleasure."

"That sounds rather old-fashioned."

"Does it? What you're not aware of is what I'm willing to do in return."

"In return?"

"I wouldn't expect a woman to give me everything she has to offer without me giving equal parts of myself. Her wants and desires will be my highest priority. I will give her the heavens if she wants them, the stars, the moon." He paused. "Then I'll take her to the depths of hell as she uncovers what sets her depraved soul free."

She shuddered.

"Can you find me all that in a *candidate,* Ms. Malloy?"

"You're rather particular."

"Indeed. I require a woman of impeccable breeding who presents her ass for my punishment when she displeases me."

The air conditioner kicked on. The whispering cool air did nothing to dissipate the heat between them.

He slid his hand around to the back of her neck, then feathered his fingers into her hair. "I want to kiss you, Ms. Malloy."

"Uhm..."

"Ask me to."

She scowled.

"I won't have you pretending that you're not curious. When you're at home this evening, by yourself with a glass of wine, horny and considering masturbating—"

"That's not me." She shook her head so fast it was obviously a desperate lie.

"No? Ms. Malloy, the room is swimming with your pheromones. Deny it." She sagged a little against his hand, and he tightened his grip on her hair, as much to offer support as to imprison her. Then he continued as if she hadn't interrupted. "You'll remember this moment, fantasize about being mine."

"No…"

"Invite me to kiss you or tell me to release you. The power is yours. Yield to temptation or leave this room wondering if it's as good as you imagine it will be."

"Mr. Sterling, this can't be happening."

Despite her protest, she didn't try to escape. "I agree. This is the first time I've had three women"—four if he counted Celeste—"attempt to force me down the aisle." He paused. "And it's the first time I've had this kind of sexual longing for an adversary. Ask me to kiss you," he repeated instead of arguing. "Be sure to say please."

"Ah…"

He loosened his grip, and she leaned toward him, keeping herself hostage. Rafe didn't smile with triumph.

"Kiss me."

"There's nothing I'd enjoy more." That wasn't the entire truth. There were a hundred things he'd like to do to her, but he made no move

Her internal standoff lasted longer than he thought it would. Excellent. She had a stubborn streak.

Hope glanced away and sighed. Then she looked at him

with clear, confident eyes. "Please kiss me."

He could drown in her and be happy about it. He captured her chin to hold her steady. On her lips, he tasted the sweetness of her capitulation. "Open your mouth, sweet Hope."

She did, and he entered her mouth, slower than he would ordinarily, softer than he would if she were his submissive.

Hope responded with hesitation, and he continued, driving deeper, seeking more. Within seconds, she yielded.

She moaned and raised onto her tiptoes to lean into him. A few seconds beyond that, she wrapped her arms around him. Hope, his adversary, had now become his willing captive.

He released her chin and moved his hand to the middle of her back, then lower to the base of her spine.

Rafe drank in the scent of her femininity. His cock surged, not from ordinary arousal, but from soul-deep recognition. Her eagerness sought the Dom in him. It took all his restraint not to press his palm against her buttocks.

Earlier he'd said she'd be thinking of him as she masturbated. The truth was, he wasn't sure how he'd banish this memory of her—strength and suppleness in one heady package.

He plundered her mouth.

She offered more until she was panting and desperate, gripping him hard.

Instead of giving in to the driving need to rip off her clothes and fuck her, he distracted himself by tugging on her hair harder. As he'd requested, her eyes were open. *So goddamn trusting.* Did she have any idea how close he was to shredding the veneer of civilization that hung between them to claim her, mark her as his?

He ended the kiss while he still could. Her mouth was swollen, and he couldn't stop staring at her lips.

Hope took tiny breaths that didn't seem to steady her. She held on to him while she lowered her heels to the floor. Then, over a few heartbeats, she dropped her hands.

"Thank you, Rafe," he prompted.

"Are you serious? I'm supposed to thank you?" She continued to look at him and undoubtedly saw his resolve.

Would she give him what he demanded? "Unless you want me to spank—"

"*Spank?*" Her chin was at a full tilt.

"Spank." He repeated with emphasis. "Unless you want me to spank your pretty little ass so hard that you can't sit down after you leave here."

"That kind of behavior is unacceptable."

"Under normal circumstances," he agreed without hesitation. "Unless you ask me for it." Part of him hoped she'd take him up on it. It would be a pleasure to prove she liked the feel of his hand on her bare skin. "I'll go first." He softened his tone, letting her glimpse his inner thoughts, a rare confession of his soul. "I enjoyed kissing you. Thank you."

"I..." She smoothed the skirt that he wanted to rip off her body.

"Look at me."

She followed his command. Then, with a soft and decidedly insubmissive tone, she said, "Thank you."

"Ms. Malloy, as I said, it was my pleasure."

Silence hung between them. Her inexperience thrilled him, and he wanted to give her another hundred firsts. Instead, he let her go. The real world—with its complex demands—was waiting. And if he wanted her at his feet, he had a lot of work to do.

"I'm not certain how much of what you said, and what we just did, is to get me to admit defeat, to quit..." She stiffened her spine.

"Maybe it started that way." His father's behavior had

pissed Rafe off, and so had his mother's ambush, even Hope herself. He'd wanted to shake her as badly as he'd been shaken. As he'd spoken to her, his desires had churned to the surface. Until now—until *her*—he had been willing to confine his kink to a club. "It didn't end that way. That I promise you."

"I will ask the candidates about their openness to your suggestions."

*Fuck.* She wanted to retreat behind a facade of business, as if their kiss hadn't changed something. "Requirements. Not suggestions. Requirements. Be clear about that. If I'm to be saddled with a woman that I don't want until death do us part, there will be none of the hysteria that my family members seem to thrive on. My *wife* will know her place and her role, and she will meet my expectations. And to be clear, she *will* ask for my kiss. Like you did." He opened the door.

Jeanine was walking toward his office with a cup of coffee, and he waved her off.

Then, voice so soft that only Hope could hear, he finished. "You have a fourteen-page interview form. I will have something similar for the women you bring to me. It will cover things such as anal play, being shared with others, edging, exhibitionism. Shall I send it to you first?"

"Please do. It will save some time in your selection process." She started past him, and he snagged her elbow.

"And Ms. Malloy? She'll fucking address me as Sir." He was unaccountably furious at her rejection. At himself. "And if you come here ever again, so will you."

Her hand trembled where she grasped her purse strap. She flicked a glance at his hand before yanking her elbow free.

**Read more of *Billionaire's Matchmaker*.**

ABOUT THE AUTHOR

I invite you to be the very first to know all the news by subscribing to my very special **VIP Reader newsletter**! You'll find exclusive excerpts, bonus reads, and insider information.

For tons of fun and to join with other awesome people like you, join my Facebook reader group: **Sierra's Super Stars**

And for a current booklist, please visit my **website**.

USA Today bestselling author Sierra Cartwright was born in England, and she spent her early childhood traipsing through castles and dreaming of happily-ever afters. She has two wonderful kids and four amazing grand-kitties. She now calls Galveston, Texas home and loves to connect with her readers. Please do drop her a note.

ALSO BY SIERRA CARTWRIGHT

**Titans**

Sexiest Billionaire

Billionaire's Matchmaker

Billionaire's Christmas

Determined Billionaire

Scandalous Billionaire

Relentless Billionaire

**Titans Quarter**

His to Claim

His to Love

His to Cherish

**Titans Sin City**

Hard Hand

Slow Burn

All-In

**Hawkeye**

Come to Me

Trust in Me

Meant For Me

Hold On To Me

Believe in Me

## Master Class

Initiation

Determination

Temptation

## Bonds

Crave

Claim

Command

## Donovan Dynasty

Bind

Brand

Boss

## Mastered

With This Collar

On His Terms

Over The Line

In His Cuffs

For The Sub

In The Den

## Collections

*Titans Series*

Titans Billionaires: Firsts

Titans Billionaires: Volume 1

*Hawkeye Series*

Here for Me: Volume One

Beg For Me: Volume Two

Printed in Great Britain
by Amazon